The Jade Head

by
Patrick Grady

To Ned Smith
with thanks for
counsel on the draft
of Jade Head. They
were very useful
Patrick Grady

Robert D. Reed Publishers • Bandon, OR

Robert D. Reed Publishers
P.O. Box 1992
Bandon, OR 97411
Phone: 650-994-6570 • Fax: -6579
E-mail: 4bobreed@msn.com
web site: www.rdrpublishers.com

Typesetter: **Barbara Kruger**
Cover Designer: **Grant Prescott**

ISBN 1-931741-44-1

Library of Congress Control Number 2004092759

Manufactured, typeset and printed in the United States of America

To my wife Jean

1

Crack went the big silver driver as it struck the small orange ball. Bob Wayne couldn't believe the power he felt pulsing up his arms as his oversized club made of the latest space-age materials smashed into the glowing little sphere. Holy shit! he thought, I've never hit a drive this hard. My game is finally starting to come together. Or maybe it's just the new club. But, what the hell, who cares as long as it's working?

Breathing in deeply, Bob took time to enjoy the sweet smell of freshly-cut grass that permeated his nostrils. But his feeling of self-satisfaction was fated to be short-lived. When he looked down the fairway of the long par-five first hole, he saw the receding tiny orange projectile hooking off deep into the thick woods on the left. Why do I always screw up? he moaned.

"Better tee up another one, Bob," his regular golf buddy Jim laughed. "And don't forget you'll be hitting three."

"Oh, go drill some rotten teeth," said Bob to his dentist friend. "I can damn well keep score myself without your help."

"Don't mind him, Jim," Carl said. "He's just sore because he's not gonna have any money left after we're done with him. He should've known better than to have agreed to play for ten dollars a hole."

"Wait a minute, here, I'm not ready to throw in the towel yet," said Bob. "I've still got my second wife and our two kids trying to cash my support checks. And then there's the car payments on that damned red Mustang convertible that you conned me into buying in a moment of mid-life weakness."

"Hell, I'll bet half the kids from Gail aren't even yours," said Sam, who was also Bob's lawyer for the messy divorce as well as the fourth member of the foursome. I shouldn't have let you agree to pay up so fast the second time. I should've made you hold out for a DNA test."

"You've been watching too much "Law & Order" on TV. We're not talking the O.J. Simpson trial here. Besides I love all the kids anyway whose ever they may be. I don't want them to think of me as a cheap bastard like my old man. He only left me with a ramshackle ole barn out in the Hollow full of empty whiskey bottles and hungry mink eating each other up. And while you all know Gail can be quite the bitch, I can't complain too much since I wasn't always a model husband myself."

"Ain't that the truth," said Carl.

The four golfing partners had grown up together in the small central Illinois town of Loganville, not far from the Indiana border. They had gone through a lot together in the first forty years of their lives. And they had few secrets from one another. In fact, nobody in the town did. Everything was an open book. That was the way it was there.

Bob teed up another brightly colored ball, his slight paunch drooping over his belt as he stooped. This time he played it safe using his old number 2 driver and pulled his swing. The ball only went a little over 125 yards, but he was relieved that at least it was on the fairway this time. Carl was up next. He hit the ball almost 250 yards using his number 1 wood.

"Look at that fucker go," he said, exuding self-satisfaction.

"You da man," said Jim.

When their turns came, Sam and Jim didn't hit as far as Carl, but at least their balls went a lot farther than Bob's. After several more lackluster shots, Bob joined the others on the green.

"You sure wreaked havoc on the grass, Bob," said Jim. "It's a wonder they still let you on the course."

"Just aerating the fairway, Jimbo. I saw you taking a pretty good divot yourself on your second shot."

Then the usual good-natured argument over the score started up. Bob claimed to be lying six, Sam and Jim five and Carl four. After a bit of badgering from Carl who always played with the intensity of the high-pressure car salesman he was by nature, Bob 'fessed up to seven strokes.

"Jesus," said Bob. "You could've at least given me the one I fanned. This isn't the Masters, you know."

"I know you for the cheatin' bastard you are. If I give you one stroke, sure as shit you'll take ten."

Since he was furthest from the hole, Bob putted first as Jim held the flag. He tapped the ball too hard and the steep downslope took it almost as far past the hole on the other side. It took two more putts to get it back up and finally in the hole. Jim and Sam only took two putts. Carl sank his for a par. His elation was hard for Bob to stomach. And this was only the beginning. It went like this or worse for seventeen more holes. Bob's low point was on the fifteenth hole where he hit two consecutive shots into the pond and Carl called him a candy ass for refusing to go into the muddy water and play one of them. Bob was mad enough to get in the water. The only thing that stopped him was that he didn't want to give Carl the satisfaction of seeing him all wet and muddy.

Back at the Nineteenth Hole in the mock Tudor clubhouse, the foursome quaffed a pitcher of ice-cold Budweiser and playfully ribbed each other as they settled their bets. Bob, who had only won two holes and was down one hundred dollars, was the big loser, and Carl, who had won eight and was up one hundred forty dollars, the grand winner. Jim and Sam were only little losers, down twenty dollars each.

"Come on, Bob, cough up," said Carl stretching his open paw across the table and rubbing his fingers together like a moneylender coming to collect.

Bob made a big deal of pulling the wallet out of his back pocket and taking out five crisp twenty dollar bills fresh from the 7-Eleven ATM. He chucked them over the table in Carl's direction like they were nothing to him.

"It wouldn't be so bad always losing to you, Carl, if you didn't look like such a geek in those godawful yellow plaid pants and that chartreuse golf shirt," he said, remarkably oblivious to his own Kelly green slacks and Day-Glo pink Lacoste shirt. "I don't know why they don't throw you out of this fuckin' country club."

"Well, at least I got in," said Carl.

Ouch! That was hitting below the belt. Bob didn't like to hear that he was the only one of the four who was not a member of the club. Twice over the years he had tried to join and been blackballed. He always blamed it on his father-in-law, his first wife Barbara's father, who had come from one of the town's fine old families. Big Pappy, as they called him, was big in more ways than one and owned a department store, a bank, some farms, and several other businesses, not all of which were inherited. Bob had gotten Barbara pregnant in high school in the back seat of the Thunderbird that Big Pappy had given her for her sixteenth birthday. Although the ole bastard would have been happy to shoot Bob and get it over with, Barbara's mother was adamant that the family honor could only be saved by a march up to the altar even if it had to be with someone like Bob from the wrong side of the tracks. So there was no real shooting, just a run-of-the-mill shotgun wedding.

The marriage into a rich and socially prominent family could have eventually enabled Bob to rise above his humble white-trash roots to reach the lofty heights of Loganville society. But living in a small bungalow bought by Barbara's family and working for a construction company owned by Big Pappy, Bob had felt trapped. It wasn't long before he walked out the door, leaving her to take care of the baby. It's no wonder Big Pappy hated him. What else could Bob have done though? How was he to know that the old man would carry such a grudge? But what really pained Bob was how they had turned his son Alan, who was now grown up, against him. If only he'd have spent some time with Alan when he was young, he had thought. He could have taken him fishing or to see a ball game, things that normal fathers do. Why was he always too busy, screwin' around with his own friends? Oh, well, it was too late now. Alan had gotten a job with General Motors after he graduated from college and moved away to Michigan. Not so far, but far enough that Bob hardly ever saw him.

Besides, Bob rationalized, he had never much liked the country club. It made him feel like a catfish out of water. Even though he had graduated from the University of Eastern Illinois, passed his exam to be a Certified Public Accountant and become a proud professional, he still felt like everyone there were looking down their noses at him. Maybe it was because they were. To them, he was still little Bobby Wayne, Jr., the son of one of the biggest drunks and losers the town had ever produced. And many believed he was likely to suffer the same fate.

The sad thing was that in his darker moments Bob feared they might be right. Sometimes he did drink a little too much. And his bad luck with women had left him with barely enough money to pay the rent on a small two-bedroom row house back behind the K-Mart. Nope, there was no way he could afford a grand, six-bedroom, estate-style house like his friends had in the Loganvale subdivision between the country club and the lake. Except maybe if he won the state lottery, or more likely robbed a bank.

Bob had not been a total wastrel, though. He had managed to sock away a little money for a rainy day. Unfortunately, it looked like the rain was starting sooner than he'd planned and it wouldn't be long before he'd be wetter than a drowned rat. Business had been bad since General Motors had shut down its central foundry, which had paid one out of every ten workers in the town a pretty good wage even if the greedy union never thought it was enough. And the little local accounting firm he worked for had stubbornly struggled to survive in a shrinking market, refusing to sell out to one of the majors seeking to establish an office in the town. The situation had finally come to a head last week. He and the two other accountants, who weren't partners in the firm, had been given their pink slips. The lump sum payment in lieu of notice wasn't much, but it was better than a kick in the ass. But not much.

What was Bob going to do now that he didn't have a job? He was afraid to admit it to himself, but he didn't have a clue. One thing he did know, though, was that he'd be damned before he'd go to work for a large accounting firm. There was no way he was going to come in every day at nine o'clock wearing a suit and tie and fill out those damn time sheets at the end of the day. Besides, why would they want to hire him anyway? In his early 40s and already washed up. Better not dwell on the negative though, he told himself, remembering something that he'd heard about the power of positive thinking from an infomercial on late-night TV while he was veging out in his chair with a can of beer in his hand. Well, at least he was still alive, and hadn't drunk himself to death like his father had done at the same age. He might as well break the news to his buddies and take his punishment like a man. Hell, he probably deserved it for being such a fool and sticking with his company all these years after the writing was already on the wall. Corporate loyalty didn't get you very far these days.

"Hey, guys! I've got some bad news that will surprise you. I've been...uh...let go this week."

"Hah! Hah! You're such an idiot, Bob, to think anyone's gonna be surprised," laughed Carl uproariously. "Everybody knows that your firm has been shutting down on the installment plan. I'm one of the few clients you have left. And it's only because I'm your good buddy and want to make sure you'll keep up your payments on that fine Mustang I sold you."

"Did you get a good severance package?" asked Sam with more concern as Bob still hadn't paid him in full for all his past legal services.

"Nope."

"Then let's sue the ass off them," the lawyer said, salivating at the prospect of a wrongful dismissal suit to relieve the tedium of his usual workload of divorces and real estate conveyances.

"Are you nuts?" asked Carl. "They're as broke as Bob."

"Without a paycheck, your creditors are gonna eat you alive. What are you gonna do?" asked Jim.

"I dunno," said Bob. "Maybe go away someplace cheap down south for a few months to see something different. Frankly, I'm downright bored with this town. Nothing ever happens here."

"It took you more than forty years to figure that out," laughed Carl. "You're a real genius."

"No, seriously, I need to put some adventure in my life," said Bob.

"Who do you think you are, Ernest Hemingway?" asked Sam.

"What's wrong with that?" asked Bob. "I've read a few of his books and he seemed to know how to live."

"The only book of his you ever read was *The Old Man and the Sea.* And that was only because Miss Brown made us read it in sophomore English. I think she picked it out because it was short and didn't use any big words."

"What are you goin' to do about Donna?" asked Jim about Donna Blake, Bob's long-time girlfriend. "You goin' to take her along?"

"I don't know. I'll have to ask, of course, but she won't want to come," said Bob. "She has her hands full with work and her mother and besides she wouldn't want to leave her kid alone. Teenage girls like Sarah can get into a lot of trouble without their mamas around to look after them. Or at least that's what Donna thinks."

"If I were you, I wouldn't take her anyway. She'd only scare away all the gorgeous, bikini-clad women that will be swarming around you when you take off your shirt at the beach and reveal your rippling muscles and six-pack," wisecracked Carl, poking Bob in his sagging stomach.

"There's only one kind of six-pack you know anything about," retorted Bob, sucking himself in. "Drink up and let's get out of here. I've got a lot of things to do now that I'm retired. I can't be wasting time hanging around with a bunch of losers like you guys."

"You gonna go to the Rotary Club meeting next Wednesday?" asked Jim.

"I don't know," said Bob. "Depends on how busy I am." Everybody laughed, causing Bob to turn red with irritation.

"You should go. It's a great opportunity to network," said Jim, using a term he had picked up from one of the high-priced management magazines he left laying around his dental office to try to attract a better-paying, business-oriented clientele. "You could send out some feelers to see if you could get any leads on a new job."

"I'll think about it," said Bob who really wanted to avoid the unpleasant reality of having to look for another job as long as possible.

2

On his way back home from the country club, Bob drove over the causeway and bridge across Lake Logan. He loved the feeling of the cool lake wind in his hair. It was almost as good as being in a speedboat flying across the lake. Maybe the flashy red convertible wasn't such a waste of money after all, he thought.

Bob then swung by one of the strip malls on Highway 1 north and pulled up in front of the First Class Travel Agency. No one could mistake it. Posters of white beaches and waving palm trees beckoned in the cracked store-front window. Getting out of his car, he sauntered in through the door. The room he entered was adorned with more exotic travel posters. A middle-aged woman with big hair and a short skirt pulled up high on her ample thigh sat behind a desk drinking a Coke and filing her nails, just passing the time hoping for someone like Bob to come through the door.

"Hi, Myrna, how's the sexiest travel agent in town?"

"I'm survivin', sweetie," she said, dropping her file and squirming to pull down her skirt in a futile attempt to look more ladylike. "What about you?"

"I need to get away from here for a while. Someplace down south in the tropics where it's always summer. Not too expensive though. I'm...er... a little short on cash these days."

"You ain't the only one, dearie, since the engine plant shut down. Well, I'll see what I can do. Let me think. What about Florida? I've got a pretty good deal on a single-wide trailer down near Englewood. You can play golf and lie on the beach to your little heart's content just like you and Donna did last year."

"Nah. I'm sick of golf and tired of Florida. Isn't there anyplace really different that you can suggest? Off the beaten track. Kinda like the places Hemingway used to hang out in."

"Well, since you asked, we just got this brochure about a place called Belize," she said, picking something up off the desk. "It might be just what you're looking for."

"Belize, never heard of it. Where the hell's that?"

"Somewhere in Central America. Says in the brochure it used to be called British Honduras."

"Let me see that," said Bob, grabbing it out of Myrna's hand. "The pictures of jungles and reefs on the cover make it look like...er...well... some kind of tropical paradise. You think it's really that beautiful or is that just your typical travel-agent hype?"

"Why don't you take the brochure home and read more about it yourself," said Myrna. "Then you can make up your own mind."

"Thanks, Myrna" said Bob, walking out of the office, reading as he went. Tripping over the door jam, he stumbled out onto the parking lot.

Bob pushed on the electrical garage door opener when he pulled into the driveway of his colonial-style row house in the less prestigious, but still respectable, north end of town. When the door opened, he drove the car into the garage. The electrical garage door was a luxury that he got after he bought the Mustang. He was afraid that without it he would have probably most of the time left the car out in the driveway at the mercy of the marauding bands of local teenagers and other vandals that ransacked the town. One expense he couldn't afford led to another, he thought. It hadn't seemed like much when he was working, but now that he didn't have a job it was going to be one more installment payment he couldn't afford.

Entering the kitchen through the door in the garage, Bob went directly to the refrigerator. Inside he didn't find much—a couple of plastic containers of left-over Chinese food, a half-eaten pizza, a carton of sour milk, some moldy cheese, and of course a half-empty case of Budweiser. I really should go shopping and stock up, he thought. Taking out one of the Chinese food containers and a bottle of Bud, he released the door, which slammed shut automatically. The shock shook the magnet off the fridge and allowed an assortment of take-out menus to flutter to the floor like a swarm of butterflies. Sitting at the stool at the counter, he gobbled the chicken fried rice right out of the container, and washed it down with ice cold beer, which was, in his limited view, the perfect beverage.

Christ, it was hot in the house, Bob thought. He went into the living room to turn the air conditioning on. The room, which could charitably only be described as suitable for a poor student or single person living on welfare, could have definitely benefited from a woman's touch. Not that Donna hadn't tried many times, only to be rebuffed before giving up. The only furniture in the room was a large sofa, a coffee table and a huge Sony television set, another of Bob's few extravagances. There was not even a rug. Instead the floor was covered with old newspapers. The dust bunny in the corner was as big as a jack rabbit. A few empty beer bottles sat on the coffee table, next to some bulging envelopes of unpaid bills

Bob's next stop, his own bedroom, was similarly decorated, or not decorated, depending on your point of view. His unmade bed was the centerpiece of the room. Dirty clothes, which didn't seem to have made it into the clothes hamper in the corner, were strewn all over the floor. The drawers of his dresser hung partially open. Another empty beer bottle sat on the bedside table.

Bob stripped off his clothes, letting them drop on his way into the adjoining bathroom. Turning the shower on, he stepped in quickly before recoiling. "Shit," he shouted, "the water is goddamn cold." Stepping back out, he let it warm up before stepping in again. "Ah!" he said as he let the hot steamy water bathe his muscles tired from eighteen holes of golf. As he got more into the groove, he began to sing an off-key version of the Beatles "Hard Day's Night," getting ever louder until the glass shower door started to vibrate in tune providing a semblance of acoustic accompaniment. When he got out, he picked a damp towel off the floor. It smelled a little musty. But, what the hell, he dried himself with it anyway, acquiring a slightly stale odor. When he was finished, he sniffed a couple of times suspiciously before reaching over, taking some Old Spice stick deodorant off the back of the toilet, and dabbing it under his arms. After wrapping the towel around his waist, he proceeded to shave and brush his teeth.

Standing right in front of the well-lit bathroom mirror, Bob inspected his face. It was burnt red from the sun he'd gotten on the golf course. His skin was kinda leathery and his wrinkles were getting deeper. A brown spot from sun damage was on the left side of his face. His eyes were bloodshot from the wind in the convertible. His wet hair looked even thinner than usual as he combed it. His pectoral and abdominal muscles looked flabby. Jesus, Bob said to himself, I really look like hell. I wonder if my life is starting to catch up with me or am I just having a bad day. They say by forty you get the face and body you deserve. But I don't think it's fair 'cause even my old man looked better than this the day he dropped dead.

Bob went back into his bedroom, and put on a clean rust-colored polo shirt and a pair of khakis and stepped into a pair of TopSiders. Casting a sideways glance at himself in the bedroom mirror as he passed, he thought, maybe I don't look so bad yet, as long as you don't get too close and I'm wearing clothes.

Bob went into the living room and sat down to look at the brochure that Myrna had given him. Belize sure looks intriguing, he thought. But he was quickly brought back to reality when he noticed the pile of bills sitting on the table next to him. Damn, he said to himself, picking up the bills, where do these all come from? The Visa bill was for $1,017 including $73.13 in interest, which took his unpaid outstanding balance up to $4,875.55. Almost maxed out, he thought. I only have a $5,000 limit on that card. He rifled through the other small bills—$245 for his quarterly property tax installment, $92.64 for home and cell telephones, $24.75 for electricity, and $22 for water. And I still have to pay Gail $900 in child support this month. Where the hell am I going to get it all? he worried. Then his eyes fixed on the travel brochure again, distracting him from the sordid details of his daily life. Belize sure looks great, he thought. Lucky I've still got another credit card I've been saving for a rainy day, he told himself.

Later that evening Bob strolled over to Donna's house as he always did. Her modest three-bedroom bungalow was only two blocks from his own. Since Donna's husband had flown the coop almost ten years ago, not much work had been done and it had gotten slightly run-down. Bob periodically tried to get the house in better shape, but he wasn't much of a handyman. More importantly, he was also a little lazy and would just as soon drink beer and watch sports on TV as work.

After he knocked softly, Toto, a prissy, miniature white poodle, came running to the door and started jumping up and down and barking furiously. Through the din, Donna yelled "Who is it?"

"It's me," said Bob. "Were you expecting one of your other lovers?"

"Don't be silly, Bob," she hollered. "Come on in."

Bob opened the door and went in. Toto continued barking and jumped up on his leg and started humping him. "Down boy, down boy," he said in his most authoritative dog-ordering voice, resisting the urge to give the horny dog a good swift kick you know where. No, don't do that, he thought. Control yourself. Donna wouldn't like that. Toto is her baby. The little yapping ball of fur ran back down the hall and into the living room. It would be nice to have a real dog like a German Shepherd or Labrador, Bob thought, as he followed Toto—one that wouldn't make him a laughingstock when he took it out for a walk, one that might be of some use for something like herding sheep or retrieving ducks.

In the living room, Bob found Donna reclining on the gold velour sofa totally absorbed in a movie magazine with Toto, tongue hanging out and panting, already back sitting next to her and eying him suspiciously. Donna was still wearing the sleeveless leopard-pattern top and black Capri pants she had worn to work that day in the beauty parlor. The light from the window shone on her medium-length, bleached-blond hair. The room was filled with the familiar sweet, musky fragrance of her Vanilla Fields perfume.

"Hi, honey, what's so interesting?"

"Hi, Bob. Take a look at this," she said, passing him the magazine. "It's about a movie they made out of a book by Frank Walsh about the Bien Lai Massacre in Vietnam. You know who he is, don't you?"

"Yeah, he was a draft dodger. A chicken-shit like him has got a lot of nerve writing about Vietnam after running away to Canada."

"Well, he's back in town now. I saw him at the Waldenbooks at the Mall signing books a couple of weeks ago. I almost bought one, but I didn't have enough money."

"That's one book I won't be buying even if I had money to waste."

"What are you talking about? You don't read books anyway."

"What do you mean? You know I've read Hemingway."

"The books you had to read in high school for book reports don't count."

"OK, what about that book I read a few years ago by what's-his-name...uh...John Grisham. Yeah, *The Firm* I think it was called. It was pretty good, too. It was all about a stupid young lawyer that got suckered into a law firm run by the Mafia and ended up in a knock-down drag-out fight for his life."

"I remember that. Are you sure we didn't see it on video?"

"No, I'm pretty sure I read it. In fact, I saw the book today. It was still lying on the floor in my bedroom, just where I threw it after I'd finished."

"Oh, brother! When are you gonna let me do something about that mess over there?"

"Don't worry. I'll eventually clean it up." Changing the subject, Bob asked, "How was your day?"

"Awful. Mrs. Hetherington made a big fuss when her hair came out a slightly different shade of brown. She accused me of using the wrong dye and refused to pay. And Ellie, who had bought the new cheap dyes to save a little money, just stood there and let me take all the flack. I felt so humiliated."

"I'm sorry, hon. I wish you didn't have to work for such a bitch," said Bob, trying to appear concerned.

"Please don't call her that. I wish I didn't have to work for her either, but there's not much else available in this town for somebody with only a high school diploma. My only chance is to catch a rich husband. Then why am I wasting my time on you? someone might ask. Not only are you not rich, but your poor track record in love suggests you're not the best marital material. At least that's what Connie says."

"Who cares what Connie says?"

"She's my best friend. We've been together since kindergarten. We even raised our kids together after our worthless husbands walked out on us at about the same time. You know she only wants what's best for me."

"Yeah, that's probably true, but she never liked me much."

"It's not that she doesn't like you. It's just that she worries about me."

"Oh, the hell with Connie! Let's escape from our problems into movieland. I've brought over a movie I stumbled on at Blockbuster when I was browsing through their old release shelves. It's called *Caribe.* It's an adventure story that takes place in a Central American country called Belize. I'll order a pizza we can eat while we watch. You still got some beer in the fridge or did Sarah and her freeloading young friends clean you out again?"

"Don't get me started on that. She's already out for the evening. Goin' to sleep over at her friend Mary's tonight. Or at least that's what she told me."

"Kids will be kids," said Bob, speaking on the basis of dated, but, no doubt still relevant, personal experience. "Better we not know what they're up to. Live and let live, I always say."

After ordering the pizza, Bob and Donna settled into their own well-worn personal grooves on the couch with Toto between them and let the movie roll. The plot of the feature attraction was pretty thin—something about CIA operatives and an arms deal with a little sex thrown in to cover all the bases and bolster the box office. Donna didn't know why, but Bob watched the second-rate flick much more attentively than usual. Well, at least he didn't fall asleep after the first half-hour. It must be a man thing, she thought. Jungles and Mayan temples had no great hold over her imagination. But inside every man there must be a little boy who wants to be Indiana Jones or Ernest Hemingway. When the pizza man arrived,

Bob was actually annoyed that he had to pause the VCR to answer the door. He must have temporarily forgotten how much he liked to wolf down pizza and guzzle beer while he watched TV, she thought.

When it was all over, Bob said, "That's quite the place. Looks a lot more exciting than here. Would you like to go there?"

"Yeah, sure, it would be fun sometime," she answered flatly.

"No, seriously, I really mean it. Would you like to go?"

"When?" she said with surprise.

"As soon as I can get the tickets. I'll call Myrna tomorrow and ask her to get them. It says on her wall 'We can get you a ticket to go anywhere, anytime.' It will be a good test for her to make sure the slogan is not just the usual commercial bullshit."

"Come on, Bob, are you out of your mind? You don't really want to go anywhere," she said, climbing over on his lap and beginning to rub his ears. "Aren't we happy enough here in our little love nest?"

"Oooh...if you put it that way...," said Bob, not wanting to spoil her mood and ruin the coming attraction.

Picking up on her cue, Bob reminded himself to go slowly. Women like it that way. Don't go in for the kill. Restraining himself, he kissed her softly on the neck until she got goosebumps. Then he caressed her body starting at her face and working downward. Next he kissed her on the lips. By the way she opened her mouth receptively, he knew that this was going to be one he wasn't going to forget. Then rude reality intruded into his fantasies. Toto began to bark wildly as he always did in these moments.

"Damn dog," said Bob, getting off the couch. He grabbed Toto roughly and carried him to the back door where he threw the growling fur ball into the yard.

"Be gentle," shouted Donna, not referring to their anticipated love-making.

Before Bob could shut the door, Toto ran over to the lawn gnome that Bob had given Donna earlier in the summer. Lifting his leg, he flashed a defiant dog smile back at Bob.

"Damn mutt," Bob muttered, shrugging.

Not being one to let a cheeky little dog get his goat for long, particularly when sexual opportunity beckoned, Bob returned to the living room where they picked up where they had left off on the couch, hardly missing a beat. They progressed to the living room floor, and then moved on to the bedroom, all the time becoming more ardent. Good thing the dog wasn't still in the room or he would go humpingly berserk, thought Bob, whose mind was still somewhat distracted by the interruption and the distant sounds of yapping. Clothes were shed en route so that by the time they reached the bed, they were both naked. While Bob's middle-aged body had seen better times, Donna was a few years younger and still reasonably fit from her regular aerobics classes in the Baptist Church basement. In the dim light of the bedroom, she looked almost perfect, at least to Bob whose close-up vision was already starting to go.

It wasn't long before they were at it hot and heavy. Back and forth, and up and down they went. Sometimes with him on top. Sometimes with her. It was kind of like a naked wrestling match without the rules and referee. Their frenzied writhing became more intense until Bob, who prided himself on his great timing, lost control and climaxed. This could have had the disastrous effect of leaving Donna unsatisfied, but Bob knew what was expected of him and hung in there long enough to finish the job by hand. It was a lesson he'd taken to heart from the parting complaint of his second wife about his deplorable inadequacy as a lover. He could still hear the laughter in the courtroom as his former wife revealed all their little marital secrets at their divorce hearing.

He knew she was finally done when the moaning stopped and her blue eyes came back into focus. "Better let the dog back in, Bob, before his barking disturbs the neighbors," she said, resuming her responsibilities as a conscientious dog owner and quiet neighbor.

Cuddling together peacefully in the bed in post-coital bliss with the white furry dog asleep on the blue fuzzy rug in the bedroom corner, Donna felt secure in her world, resting comfortably in the thought that she had once again tamed Bob using the oldest female trick in the book. What she didn't know was that this was only wishful thinking on her part. In spite of her years, she still hadn't learned that men will pretend to go along with almost anything women propose in return for sex. Once satisfied, though, it's quite a different story. They do whatever they damn well please. And that is exactly what Bob was already planning to do. While he hadn't yet found the required excuse, his bags were already packed in his mind.

It had been almost a month since Bob had seen his two youngest children. He wished he could just drop over for a visit. But relations between him and Gail were tense at best. Better give her a call and try to arrange something, he thought.

"Hello, Gail, it's Bob."

"Whaddaya want?" she replied icily.

"To see the kids, same as always. I'd like to take Ben and Jen out this weekend for a hamburger and maybe play miniature golf or go bowling or something."

"I'm sorry, but the twins are awfully busy with all their activities. And Dave said he might take them out in the boat."

"Cut the crap," said Bob, bristling at the mention of Dave. "They're my kids, not his, and I have a right to see them. It says so right in our child support agreement."

"Why your sudden interest in playing the good father?"

"Haven't I always been a good father? I come over and see them every couple of weeks and always give them little presents for their birthday and Christmas."

"If you've been such a 'good father,' how come Matt hardly ever goes to see you when he comes home from college?"

"Er...you know damned well you turned him against me. You told him a lot of bad things about me."

"I didn't have to. He saw how swollen my face was that time you hit me."

"You're not gonna bring that up again. That was when I got drunk after I learned about you and Dave."

"For a while you drank quite a lot, didn't you? Kinda like that drunken womanizing bum you called Dad."

"And I suppose Dave is a saint."

"No, certainly not, but he's a helluva big improvement over you...in all respects, if you get my drift," she sneered.

"I'm not gonna argue with you anymore," said Bob, trying hard to control his anger. "I got my fill of that when we were married. Just answer my question. Can I see the kids this weekend or not?"

"No, we've already got plans. Call me again next week and maybe we can arrange something. Oh, and by the way, I haven't received your child support check yet this month. I suppose it's in the mail as usual?"

"All right, if you want to be that way," said Bob, slamming down the receiver, his face red with rage.

3

The regular Wednesday weekly luncheon meetings of the Rotary Club were held in the main dining room of the historic old Loganville Lincoln Hotel. Standing before Old Glory with his hand over his chest, Dick Black, the president, opened the meeting by leading the members in that grand American custom of reciting the *Pledge of Allegiance.* "I pledge allegiance to the flag of the United States of America, and to the Republic for which it stands, one nation under God, indivisible, with liberty and justice for all," everyone mumbled in unison just like they used to do in school. Perhaps, they found it reassuring that some things still seemed to be the same even if they weren't.

Next came the not-so-ecumenical prayer. "God, Our Father in Heaven, we thank you for the opportunity to serve you through Rotary and for the good friendship and fellowship it offers us. We ask your blessing on all our efforts. We also thank you for this food and ask your blessing on it. In the name of Jesus we do pray," intoned Mike Renn, taking his turn at prayer duties. "Amen," came the dutiful reply from everyone, including Bob Wayne, who hadn't been in a church since his second wedding which took place in a non-denominational wedding chapel run quite profitably by a defrocked local Evangelical Minister.

Mary Hawkins, who got to choose the songs, led the room in an incongruous medley of *Give My Regards to Broadway* and *R-O-T-A-R-Y,* the Rotary's own stirring song. It may have been corny, but that didn't stop everyone from really cutting loose. The strange thing about singing is that the song doesn't matter much. It's the singing itself that brings people together and leaves them feeling all fuzzy and warm. Bob instinctively knew this and his own enthusiastic off-key voice resonated above the others.

No sooner did the singing stop than shifts of blue-uniformed waitresses wearing white aprons started serving the food. "Not that rubbery chicken again," groaned Carl.

"I don't care," said Bob. "I didn't have any breakfast this morning. I'm so hungry I'd eat a horse."

"Didn't Donna feed you this morning?" asked Carl.

"You may not have noticed with your wife staying at home and waiting on you hand and foot," said Bob, "but women don't make breakfast anymore. It's everyone for themselves when I sleep over at Donna's."

"I don't know why you're wasting time talking to us here, Bob," interrupted Jim. "If I were you, I'd be over there schmoozing with Larry Robinson. He's a senior partner in Young & Anderson, you know."

"You think I don't know who he is?" Bob huffed.

"Well, did you ever talk to him?"

"Er...not really."

"Now is a good time to start. He might give you a job if you weren't so obviously stupid as well as obnoxious."

"Say, why don't you guys give me a break? I'd like to eat my lunch in peace," pleaded Bob.

After lunch, the first item of business was the announcement of birthdays. Bob and Carl clapped especially loudly and hooted rowdily when Jim's name was announced. This was to embarrass him as he was sitting right between them at the table and the noise caused everyone to look. Then came the introduction of guests. No one except a real estate agent and insurance broker from neighboring towns out prospecting for business. Hardly worth mentioning, Bob thought, kind of like himself if he ever visited one of their clubs.

The President announced that their next week's speaker would be John McComb, their local Republican Congressman.

"Not him again," groaned Jim who was a Democrat. "Why do they always ask him?"

"Could be that he's the only Congressman we've got," replied Carl.

"Well, at least once I'd like to hear a Democrat speak," sulked Jim.

"First you've got to get one elected. You know that there hasn't been a Democrat elected in this District since the Civil War," laughed Carl who was a Republican precinct committeeman.

The President continued with an update on the club's community service activities: a youth exchange with a town in Germany, a scholarship to the best student graduating from Loganville High School, and the clean-up of Jackson Park. Carl and Bob whispered back and forth as the meeting droned on, just like they used to do in school, becoming increasingly raucous as they argued about one thing and then another. That is until the President introduced the guest speaker. He was an orthopedic surgeon named Dr. Jack Sherman who had worked on a project sponsored by their fellow Rotarians from Southern Illinois. It brought crippled Belizean children to a local hospital for orthopedic surgery.

"Shh! Carl, I want to hear this," said Bob, suddenly becoming interested in what was being said.

Taken aback that, for the first time in living memory, Bob actually wanted to listen to the official speaker, Carl sulked silently as Dr. Sherman took the podium. The good doctor was wearing a khaki suit and sporting a trim salt and pepper beard, which gave him a rugged, outdoorsy look kind of like a young Papa Hemingway. "Thanks, Dick, for your kind introduction," he said in a voice that sounded to Bob like the preacher at a revival his father had taken him to as a boy during one of the old reprobate's brief sober periods when he was looking for Jesus to save him from himself. "It's a real pleasure to be here today with my fellow Rotarians from Loganville to tell you all about the Belizean Crippled Children's Project and hopefully to enlist your support. Since 1977, we have been sending orthopedic surgeons like myself to Belize every year to run free clinics for children with physical deformities. Through these clinics we have helped thousands of children, most from families too poor to afford medical care. And we have brought more than 150 children that we couldn't help in the clinics to the Shriner's Hospital in East St. Louis for sophisticated corrective surgery that wasn't available in Belize. While in the United States, the children and their parents have been guests in our homes. We have become very attached to them and have been fortunate to share their happiness in overcoming their physical disabilities. Today I've brought a short video we made to show you more about our project. Featured in the video is the story of Pedro Uck, a young Mayan boy whose foot had to be amputated when gangrene set in after he cut himself with a machete. After being fitted with a prosthesis as a result of our program, he was able to live a more normal life. Now that he has grown up, he has become a grade school teacher and is giving back to his own people. Enough said, let's start the film."

On cue, the lights dimmed and a picture came up on the big screen TV in the front of the room. The video showed not only the clinics and the children, but provided a background travelogue on the country.

While Bob was not unmoved by the disabled children, he was again mesmerized by the exotic images of a country that was so close to America yet so different. As he watched, he again felt a very strong desire to hike in the jungle and explore a Mayan temple for himself. That would sure beat hanging around Loganville, he thought, waiting for all his creditors to descend upon him like vultures. It would be a real adventure.

When the video was over, Dr. Sherman asked if anybody had any questions. A few hands went up. The questions were the ordinary ones that might be expected following such a presentation. How long were you down there? What did you do? Where did you stay? How were the people? What was the country like? What do they eat down there? But, to Bob, Dr. Sherman's answers were extraordinary, displaying a missionary zeal for the project and all things Belizean. Bob could contain his own enthusiasm no longer. Like someone induced to testify for the Lord at a revival meeting, he raised his hand and asked, "If I were to go down to Belize, is there anything an accountant like myself could do to help you out?"

After pensively stroking his beard a few times, Dr. Sherman replied with the obvious "Why, sure. If you're really an accountant, you could always take a look at our books for us. The volunteers who have gone down to Belize on our project so far have been mostly doctors, like myself, and nurses. Keeping the books hasn't been much of a priority with so many needy children to be looked at. I'm afraid we may have been a bit too casual. We could certainly use some help from a professional like yourself to get prepared in case we ever get audited by the IRS. Yeah, for sure, give me a call if you decide to go and we can set something up."

"I'll do that," said Bob, thinking to himself that their books must be a real disaster, worse even than some of the charities he's audited in Loganville and they were pretty bad.

Turning to Carl, who was still speechless and looking at him like he had gone crazy, Bob said, "This gives me just the excuse I've been looking for to go to Belize and escape my creditors at the same time. How could Donna complain about me going down there for such a worthy cause? It would also be a good way to meet some people once there."

"Lose your job, and you're going off to help crippled children. Are you nuts?" asked Carl.

"No, just bored and besieged by my creditors," said Bob.

"Fine," said Carl. "You can go off to hell for all I care. And I suspect it wouldn't be much hotter than Belize. I'll bet in the heat you won't be playing much golf down there, that is, if they even have any courses in such a godforsaken out-of the-way place."

"There's more to life than playing golf," Bob replied philosophically.

"Like what, for instance?" asked Carl.

By this time, Bob wasn't listening anymore. In his mind he was already in Belize.

A few days later, Bob called Dr. Sherman and told him he had definitely decided to go to Belize. Dr. Sherman sounded very pleased. He said he would let the local Rotary Club in Belize City know that Bob was coming. They could tell him exactly what sort of accounting help was needed when he got there.

Donna was really excited. Bob had invited her to go to Indiana Beach for the weekend. She hadn't been there since she was a little girl and she remembered it as being a magical place, kind of a poor man's Disneyland for small-town Hoosiers. Bob knew that Indiana Beach was a special place for her, she thought. Maybe he was taking her there to propose. That would be, ooh...sooo romantic!

Early in the morning before it got hot, Bob picked Donna up in his red Mustang. Country music was blaring on the radio from WLOG. It was Shania Twain singing "Any Man of Mine."

"This is one of my favorite songs," said Donna, climbing over the door into the car and beginning to sing along to the music.

When the song ended, Bob said, "This is the first time I've ever paid any attention to the words of this song. And you know, I don't like them very much. They offend my delicate male sensibilities. I hope you don't expect me to be like that."

"Sure would be nice," she said. "But realistically, nope, I have set more modest objectives, which for the present must remain confidential for strategic reasons."

What the hell is she talking about? Bob thought, but was afraid to ask.

All the way there, driving with the top down, the refreshing wind kept them cool. Donna was glad she'd brought a scarf to keep her hair from getting too windblown. The countryside was flat as a pancake and covered in corn and soybeans as far as the eye could see. The corn was already higher than an elephant's eye. The crop report on the radio confirmed that it was going to be a bumper year. This was a country made to drive in. The road was straight and the traffic was sparse. With

Indiana Beach beckoning, he put the pedal to the metal and the speedometer settled in above 90.

As the car whizzed by a series of Burma-Shave-type signs, Bob read aloud, "Roses are Red...My Gun is Blue...I am safe...How about YOU?"

"I forgot mine," he joked. "What about yours?"

"It's in the drawer at home next to the bed where I always keep it in case I ever catch you cheatin'," she deadpanned.

"I better not mess," he said, not sure if she was joking.

Upon arrival, Bob took Donna to check in at the Beach House Inn within the Beach grounds. The room was a double with a king bed. This must be something really special, thought Donna. When we go anywhere, Bob always stays in cheap roadside motels; you know, the ones with stained, lumpy mattresses, and rooms that stink of smoke and have fist-shaped holes in the wall.

After they had settled in, they went for a walk along the boardwalk. It was smaller and tackier than Donna had remembered, but it still evoked her strong childhood feelings of awe. People of all ages and sexes were walking back and forth in everything from swimming suits to sundresses and jeans, revealing sunburnt bodies of all sizes and shapes. Many of the bodies were adorned with tattoos, ranging from the new trendy tribal bands and oriental letters to old-fashioned skeleton-and-devil motifs favored by local motorcycle clubs. And many had piercings. Those on women's navels caught Bob's eye as if an invitation to take a look at a nice, flat, tanned stomach. Those on men's nipples were something else and gave Bob a twitch of pain.

Stands were selling cotton candy, flavored ice, and salt water taffy. The deep-fat fryers in the boardwalk restaurant cooking French fries and pogos gave off the pungent odor of burning oil. Callers touted carnival games—shooting, throwing rings, baseball tossing. Souvenir shops offered T-shirts, towels, and hats. Donna dragged Bob into one selling knickknacks.

"Aren't these frogs cute," said Donna, picking up and closely examining a stuffed frog playing the banjo. It was one of a set of frogs involved in every conceivable legal non-sexual recreational activity from bowling to beer drinking.

"Ugh!" said Bob who abhorred kitsch almost as much as Donna adored it.

When Bob walked out the door, he stepped on a discarded cotton candy cone. Some of the candy stuck on the sole of his shoe. He shuffled as they walked down the boardwalk trying to rub it off. With each step he could feel himself sticking to the wood underneath, but the attachment grew less and less as they progressed. Bob was finally able to scrape it off on the bottom rung of the fence separating the boardwalk from the water as Donna amused herself throwing food pellets from the vending machine to the hundreds of carp that swarmed in the water below. When she was finished, they resumed their progress on the board walk.

"Look, Bob, there's the Giant Gondola Wheel." said Donna, jumping up and down with the excitement of a child. "I used to love that as a kid. Let's take a ride, please, please."

"Okay, okay, as long as you don't make me go on one of those roller coasters " said Bob.

"I promise," said Donna.

In spite of its imposing size, the ride wasn't particularly thrilling, which suited Bob just fine given his fear of heights. Sitting in the gondola car suspended from the giant Ferris wheel, they held hands and enjoyed an eagle's eye view of the lake and amusement park as Donna relived one of the greatest thrills of her girlhood.

Next, for a few hours of swimming and sunbathing, Bob and Donna went to the misnamed Sand Beach, which is really a huge enclosed swimming pool jutting out into the lake and surrounded by sand. The lake itself was apparently too dirty to swim in, legal liabilities for resort owners being what they are. Bob and Donna took turns applying fragrant, coconut-smelling sun tan lotion onto each other. Their lazy summer afternoon was only broken by a few trips to the boardwalk for cold drinks and the customary greasy beach eats. A more relaxing way to spend a day waiting for Bob to pop the question would have been hard for Donna to imagine.

That evening Bob and Donna got all dressed up to go out for dinner. Donna wore her yellow sundress adorned with big white daisies and Bob had on his chinos and a blue and red Tommy Hilfiger sport shirt. Bob had made reservations for the Skyroom Restaurant, which was situated in a glass-enclosed room on top of the largest building on the boardwalk. There, enjoying the panoramic view of the lake, they dined on prime rib, roast potatoes and green beans. Bob, who ordinarily was a beer man, ordered a bottle of medium-priced California Cabernet Sauvignon to try to make the occasion more elegant. A classic rock band played in the background. Before dessert, the band began to play their song, "Donna" by Ritchie Valens, which Bob had secretly requested on a trip to the washroom. He asked Donna to dance. Once on the floor, she snuggled up closely, put her head on his shoulder and began stroking his neck with her hand. This couldn't be more perfect, Donna purred to herself.

While they were eating their dessert, they watched a fireworks display over Shafer Lake. Then the big moment Donna had been waiting for came.

"Donna, there's something I've been wanting to talk to you about," said Bob, leaning over the table and looking right in Donna's eyes.

"Yes, Bob," she said, looking back intently, her blue eyes filled with keen anticipation.

"I've decided for sure I'm gonna go to Belize."

"What?" she said, her eyes widening.

"I'm going to Belize. I'm gonna provide some accounting help to the Rotary Club's project down there for crippled children."

"Crippled children? For God sake, Bob, what about us?" she asked, her eyes narrowing.

"Whaddaya mean?" he asked with a genuine surprise that could only be rooted in his colossal insensitivity.

"I thought you brought me here to ask me to marry you," she said, starting to cry.

"Oh!" he said, finally realizing that he was indeed in deep shit.

"Don't you think I'm good enough for you?" she sobbed.

"No, no, ...you know that's not it."

"Then what?"

"I'm just...er...not ready, I guess."

The spell was broken. If it wasn't so far, Donna would have insisted that Bob take her straight home. He wouldn't pass go and he certainly wouldn't be collecting anything. As it turned out, Bob needn't have splurged on a king size bed that night. He ended up sleeping on the couch and was lucky she didn't make him sleep in the car. As he laid there trying to go to sleep, he wondered if she really had a gun in the drawer of her bedside table. Nah, she was just kidding, he told himself.

4

On an overcast morning, a few days later, Donna reluctantly drove Bob to the Loganville Municipal Airport to catch a plane. It was an old PWA airport nestled among the flat cornfields. In its day, transcontinental flights en route to New York or Los Angeles used to stop for refueling and to pick up passengers. For people who grew up in Loganville, it had been a romantic window on the wider world where people flew from coast to coast and dined on fine china at ten thousand feet. Now it was only for private planes and commuter flights to Chicago—not the stuff of dreams, even in Loganville.

The daily flight would get him to O'Hare Airport in less than an hour, then he'd catch an American Airlines flight to Miami that would connect him with another to Belize City. If all went according to plan, he'd be in a hammock on the beach at Ambergris Caye, sipping a planter's punch by sunset. Dreaming that all his troubles would be far away, at least for a while anyway, he was really feeling upbeat. Donna, on the other hand, hadn't recovered from the Indiana Beach fiasco and was still kind of down. She didn't want him to go and was suspicious about his eagerness to leave her. She wasn't buying his excuse that he was going to help out a Rotary Club project for crippled children. It was out of character for him. He wasn't really that nice. Something must be up. Her attitude toward Bob was cold and he could feel the ice.

"Cheer up. I'm not going away forever," he said as they turned off the main highway on to the Airport Road.

"I can't help it, Bob. I have strange feeling about this trip. It's as if you're slipping away from me."

"Nonsense, I just need a change for a while and the chance to help out with the Rotary Club project is a great opportunity," he said, still sticking to his fishy story. "I've lived in this town too long. I've always done the same things. And I'm not getting any younger. If I'm ever gonna try something different, I have to do it now." This was closer to the truth.

"It scares me when you talk like that. I feel like I don't really know you. I wish you could just be happy here with me. You get along so well with Sarah, too. She actually talks to you, which is more than she does with me. We could make a real good family."

"Maybe, ...er...when I get back."

"That is, 'if you come back.' I think you're running away from me as much as from anything else in this town, but you're afraid to admit it even to yourself."

Bob didn't have any comeback because there was an element of truth in what she said. Anything he could think of sounded empty and not very reassuring. So he just continued to drive in silence, trying to think of something comforting to say.

When Bob pulled up in front of the terminal, he leaned over and put his arm around Donna. Wanting to leave her on a more upbeat note, he tried to reassure her. "Don't worry, honey, I'll be back," he said, kissing her farewell. "And while I'm gone, we can keep in touch. I promise I'll call."

Handing Donna the keys to the Mustang, he said, "Take good care of it. It's my baby. As long as you've got it, you'll know I'm coming back."

Donna stared at the keys and the horseshoe shaped key ring, before dropping it kerplunk in her purse.

Bob got out of the car and got his huge bag out of the trunk. As he pulled it into the terminal, he turned and smiled and waved. Donna worried this was good-bye forever and sobbed softly. Bob looked too happy to be leaving to her. Sure he might come back, she thought, but it wouldn't be the same. She waited in the parking lot for twenty minutes until the plane took off before she mustered up the strength to return home to walk Toto and to prepare for another stressful day of work at the beauty parlor.

The flight on the little commuter plane was uneventful. It took less than an hour to get to Chicago and the aircraft touched down on schedule. As the plane taxied up to the terminal, Bob looked out the window at the many Boeing 747 and Lockheed 1011 jumbo jets parked on the tarmac. His own tiny plane looked like a toy in comparison. Similarly, O'Hare Airport dwarfed the Loganville Municipal Airport. After disembarking, Bob had plenty of time to make his connections. This was fortunate as he had to go all the way from one end of O'Hare to the other, schlepping his very heavy bag. He was hurrying to check the bag and clear security. Even though Bob had been at O'Hare many times before, he still felt overwhelmed by the sheer size of the terminal and its incredible hustle and bustle.

The departure lounge at the gate for American Airlines Flight 2213 to Miami was so crowded that Bob had trouble finding a seat. The only ones available were way in the back. Bob took a seat and tried to read a newspaper. When he heard the pre-boarding announcement, he jumped right up and headed for the gate along with everybody else. He needn't have bothered. When he got there, he had to stand around some more while people traveling with small children and others needing assistance and business class passengers boarded. Finally, the economy passengers like Bob were allowed on by row numbers starting at the back. As Bob's seat was in row 7, this meant still more thumb twiddling. By the time Bob finally got on the 737 that was going to take him to Miami, he was just happy to take his seat. He didn't even mind when he had to undo his seatbelt and get up to let an elderly couple climb in to take their seats near the window. As soon as the plane was in the air, he ordered a double Scotch on the rocks. This put him in a mellow mood that made the two-hour flight go more quickly. That was good as there wasn't much to eat other than a hard, cold ham sandwich and candy bar in a clear plastic container. Oh well, at least he would be able to catch a few winks during the movie. It turned out to be an old one called *Passenger 57* about an international terrorist that hijacks an airplane on which a security expert happens to be traveling. One particularly loud scene interrupted his slumber. Bob awoke just in time to see the Wesley Snipes' character engaged in a knock-down-drag-out fight with the hijacker who he finally succeeds in throwing out of the plane. They really ought to screen their movies more closely, he thought, suspiciously looking around the plane at the other passengers. Every time he was about to fall asleep afterwards, he kept jerking himself awake overcome by the sensation of falling through empty space.

When Bob emerged into the Miami International Airport, still groggy from his nap, he felt like he was already in Latin America. He was surrounded by a crowd of people. It was almost as large as in Chicago, but much more colorfully dressed. He strained his ears and could hear that most of them were speaking Spanish. This was a language he had studied for two years in high school, yet only understood a little, and only then when people spoke slowly and enunciated clearly. Unfortunately, this was something which native Spanish speakers seemed congenitally unable to do even when speaking to a small child. Even the announcements over the PA system in Miami were in Spanish as well as English. At least Belize is an English-speaking country, he thought, even if this part of the United States isn't anymore.

Bob had tight connections so he went straight to the gate where people were already queuing up. Many of them were Belizeans laden down with boxes and bags of goods they had purchased in the United States. With their CD players and portable TV sets, they were stretching the definition of carry-on baggage to the absolute limit. For many of the younger single men predominantly making up the crowd, these electronic devices were the trophies earned from back-breaking stints as seasonal workers in the Florida citrus groves and horticultural fields. Admiring friends and family would be waiting to meet them at the airport to see who would bring home the biggest or the best prizes. There were also a lot of tourists lining up for the flight. Or at least they looked to Bob like tourists with their sandals, shorts, T-shirts and large hats.

In the crowd, Bob noticed a family that looked different than the other passengers. It included a man, a woman, and six children ranging in age from an infant to teenagers. All were fair-skinned and blond. The man was dressed in an old-fashioned-looking black suit and had on a straw hat. The woman wore a long plain dress and bonnet and cradled a baby in her arms. The boys were dressed like their father and the girls like the mother. It reminded Bob a little bit of the way people dressed in the Amish town of Arthur southwest of Loganville—a throwback to pioneer times when life was simple and morals strict, not like today when anything goes.

The boarding announcement was made in both English and Spanish. Before long all the merchandise and people, including Bob, were crammed into American Airlines Flight 2193 and were more or less happily on their way to Belize City.

5

Looking out the window of the 737 as it touched down at the Phillip Goldson International Airport in Belize City, Bob saw the remains of the old British Air Base complete with anti-aircraft gun emplacements and camouflage netting. Bob felt as if he were landing in some kind of a guerrilla base. The plane taxied up to a seedy-looking terminal that wasn't much larger than the Loganville Municipal Airport, a fact which shouldn't have been surprising given the relative size of the two towns. Bob deplaned and followed the other passengers across the tarmac to clear Customs and Immigration. It was so hot that the tar under his feet had melted and stuck like toffee to his shoes as he walked. The sun beat down and the ripe, almost rotten, smell of tropical vegetation filled his nostrils with every breath.

The arrival of his flight was the big event of the day for the Customs and Immigration inspectors working at the airport. The 150 or so passengers on his plane interrupted what must have otherwise been a lazy day as they crowded into the room and separated into three lines waiting to be processed. Bob quickly cleared passport control where a lethargic young man in a khaki uniform took the entry card he had filled out on the plane and mechanically stamped his passport. No problem. Bob then went over and joined the crowd milling around the conveyer belt at the end of the room waiting for their bags. Once he got his bags, he went to Customs. There were some Belizeans ahead of him in the line animatedly arguing with the beleaguered inspector about something or other. Next came some tourists who meekly submitted to the procedures. Finally Bob's turn came and he too put his bags on a table and dutifully opened them, just like he saw everyone else doing. The inspector reached into the bag and felt around, pawing all Bob's underclothes with what Bob viewed as an excessive, if not perverted, zeal. Finally, having had his fun, the inspector told Bob to close the suitcase and flagged him through. Welcome to Belize! Bob thought.

Bob's ordeal was not over yet. He still had to contend with a crowd of taxi drivers and porters trying to grab his bag and take him into Belize City. This would have been all right, except for the minor detail that he didn't want to go to Belize City. He was actually trying to go out to Ambergris Caye. When Bob told this to one of the drivers, he was directed through a small door back into the terminal to catch the Tropic Air flight to San Pedro. When he got up to the counter, he was in luck. The flights left every hour on the half hour just as Myrna had told him. In fact, one was leaving in ten minutes. He had just enough time to pick up a guidebook at the airport gift shop, which was definitely something he was going to need. His first glance at Belize from the limited perspective of the airport was all it took to convince him that he was definitely in terra incognito and that his small-town, downstate-Illinois coping skills were not going to get him very far.

When Bob returned to the gate, the passengers were already filing through the door to walk out to the Cessna Caravan sitting on the runway. As the plane only had 14 seats, counting the pilot's, every available one had to be used. Curious to see how you actually flew a small plane, Bob climbed into the front seat right next to the pilot. He was a young Latino Belizean who must have been in his mid-twenties and was wearing a crisply-ironed, white, short-sleeved, uniform shirt, blue pants, and, of course, aviator sunglasses. The pilot powered up the engine and taxied out to the end of the runway. Turning back down the main runway, he gunned the throttle with gusto. With an almost deafening roar, the plane lurched and headed down the runway. It quickly gathered speed and was airborne in seconds, leaving much of the noise behind. It flew out over the water and headed northeast toward the keys.

Within minutes, they were flying 2,000 feet over the turquoise water, low enough for a spectacular view of the fishing boats and reefs below. Passing over a barrier reef island, Bob could see palm trees and a couple of shacks. The next thing he knew they were coming into San Pedro on Ambergris Caye. On the approach into the San Pedro Airport, Bob saw the outline of a crashed plane under the water in the mangrove swamp at one end of the runway. He could also see the little village looming up right at the other end. Between the swamp and the town, it didn't look like there was much room to land. But the pilot, who must have landed here several times a day, every day for years, handily put the plane down and pulled over nicely at the end of the runway with at least ten feet to spare before he would've hit the short wooden fence separating the airport from the nearby houses. The whole flight lasted a scant 20 minutes from take-off to landing, but it had transported Bob to another, slower-paced world.

Bob got out of the plane and walked across the white sand to wait for his bag outside of the one-room wooden terminal building, which was shaded by coconut palm trees. A man from Wally's Villa Resort was already there waiting for him just as Myrna had promised. He was an older Mexican-looking hombre in a T-shirt and shorts and no shoes. His white shirt was emblazoned with "You'd better Belize it" in red letters. When the bags arrived, Bob pointed his out. The man dutifully picked it up and put it in a golf cart, the stand-in for cars on this tiny peaceful island, and took him to the hotel, if that was what you could call it. The small wooden building, surrounded by a collection of six palapas, or thatch huts, sat right on the beach about a quarter mile south of the air strip. As they went around the building to its main entrance on the beach side, the salty breeze coming off the sea was invigorating. The man escorted Bob into the office where he was greeted by the proprietor himself who was relaxing in a lounge chair At the man's side was an end table covered with books and magazines, and empty glasses. A mounted tarpon game fish and a kitschy carved coconut head hung on the wood-paneled wall behind him. A small air conditioner hummed rhythmically in the window.

Wally was a portly American in his early sixties. His brown hair was slicked back over his bald spot, and his nose was large and red. He wore owl-shaped glasses which magnified his friendly blue eyes. In a Hawaiian shirt and loose-fitting white slacks and sandals, he looked very Belize.

"Welcome to my hotel, Mr. Wayne," he said, waddling out of his chair and reaching out to shake Bob's hand. "I'm Wally Sinclair."

"Pleased to meet you, Mr. Sinclair."

"Oh! Just call me Wally. We're not formal in Belize as you'll soon find out. You must be parched after your long journey. Would you join me for a drink while Manuel takes your bag to your room?"

"Sure. Whaddaya have?"

"Every day at this time, I have a piña colada or two. Would that suit you?" Wally said.

"That would be excellent."

Wally reached into a small fridge to pull out a pitcher of milky-looking juice. He then took two glasses off the shelf and mixed the contents of the pitcher with a healthy shot of rum from a bottle he kept stashed behind the counter. Giving Bob one of the glasses, Wally motioned for him to sit down in the chair next to his own. As soon as Bob was seated, Wally plopped back down into his own chair with a big shit-eating grin on his face. He had Bob just where he wanted him, a guest with whom he could share drinks and swap stories.

A big orange tomcat slunk out of the back room and jumped up on Wally's lap. He began to purr as Wally stroked his ears. "Hi, Ernest, nice pussy," Wally said.

"That cat has six toes on its front feet," said Bob.

"Yes," said Wally. "It's a polydactyl cat I picked up on a trip to Key West. They raise them there at the Hemingway House. Descended from Ernest Hemingway's cats—that's why I call him Ernest. He's my own little living connection to literary history. And he's also pretty good at catching mice."

"Well, I'll be damned," said Bob.

"What brought you down here?" Wally asked, continuing to pet the cat.

"Well, Belize seemed like a good place to get away from it all for a while. What about you? How'd you end up running a hotel down here?"

"I came on vacation about ten years ago with my wife Mabel, God rest her soul. This hotel was for sale. The previous owner had managed to drink himself into personal and financial oblivion. I was about ready to retire from my law practice anyway since I had come into a little money. So I said, what the hell, and bailed him out and bought it. I've been here ever since trying to avoid his fate. I haven't made much money from it, but I get by. And who could complain about the life style? I sure hope it stays like this. But I'm a little worried after all the publicity we got from that show *Temptation Island.* Did you see it?"

"No, I'm afraid I didn't."

"Well, you didn't miss much. It was one of the first of those new reality shows made by Fox—kind of real life soap opera where a lot of scantily clad young people ran around Captain Morgan's and the Mata Chica Resort trying to bed each other's partners. They're trying to turn love and sex into a spectator sport, you know. What next? Will we be watching people die in hospitals?"

"Sounds pretty kinky. Other than that, whaddaya do around here?" laughed Bob.

"We're doing it right now as we speak," said Wally, toasting Bob with his drink.

"Besides this, I mean."

"Ah! The most popular things are fishing and snorkeling or diving. There are plenty of boats you can charter to go out to the reef and beyond. You can fish or snorkel or whatever you want to do. When you get tired of that, you can get a boat to take you up the New River to see the Mayan Ruins at Lamanai. If you want a little more night life than the handful of local restaurants and bars offer, you can go over to Belize City for some real excitement. It's only a short plane or speedboat ride away...."

The cat jumped down when Wally was interrupted by the entrance of a white-featured, but darkly-tanned, mulatto with large, flat, bare feet from a lifetime of walking on sand without shoes. Like most people on the island, he was wearing shorts and a T-shirt. His reddish dreadlocks fell over his shoulders, making him look like a friendly lion.

"Hi, Wally, maan, you mek Happy Hour widout mi," he asked.

"No, only providing some liquid refreshment for my new friend, Bob, who just arrived from the States," replied Wally. "Bob, I'd like you to meet Gideon Wallace. He's descended from the English pirate, Captain Peter Wallace, himself. That old buccaneer settled on these islands more than three hundred years ago so that he could help himself to the treasures of passing Spanish galleons. Belize was named after him, you know. It doesn't sound much like Wallace but they tell me it is. Pronunciations and spellings change over time, you know, maybe more here than elsewhere. Anyway, if there's anything you want to do out on the water, Gideon's your man."

"Dis Wally, e some tang too. E can skin a dog wid e tongue."

"It's the lawyer that's still in me," said Wally humbly, bowing slightly to Gideon. "Can I offer you a drink, Gideon?"

"No, maan. Gotta tek bacras fishin dis nite. Wesa se'ya latah," he said.

"See you tomorrow, Gideon," said Wally. Gideon left as quickly as he had come.

"What the hell was he saying?" asked Bob.

"Don't worry. You'll learn to understand Gideon soon enough," said Wally. "He speaks what they call Creole. It's a pidgin that combines a mostly English vocabulary with African syntax and grammar. The early slaves made it up to communicate with their English masters."

"By the way, to let you in on a little local lore, you may be interested to learn that the relationship between slaves and their masters was different in Belize than elsewhere. There were no big plantations here like in the Caribbean islands. The slaves used to work in the bush instead. A white overseer would take a small gang of slaves up a river to a bush camp where they would stay for a few weeks or even months to harvest logwood or mahogany trees. The slaves all had an ax or a machete and a few even had muskets. If the white overseer wanted to get back to Belize City with a good load of lumber, he'd better not act like Simon Legree or he'd end up like Stonewall Jackson, dead with a bullet in the back. No, the blacks in Belize were never intimidated by whites like they were in some of the islands. From the start, there was more of an equal relationship here, even if they were still slaves."

As Bob was to learn, Gideon was only one of a number of colorful island characters that regularly popped in and out to pay homage to Wally as he held court in one of his two identical floral-cushioned lounge chairs—one in the office and one on the porch. Another regular in Wally's salon was the Alcalde, or Mayor, Estevan Palacio, a five-foot tall mestizo who knew the business of everybody on the island, particularly around election time. The town's one policeman, Juan Garcia, who looked like his portly namesake on the old TV version of Zorro, also stopped by for an occasional cocktail and to discuss which local troublemakers needed to be given a free trip to the mainland to prevent them from spoiling the island's tourist trade.

Over the next week, Bob got to know Wally pretty well. He easily fell into Wally's lazy lifestyle of sleeping late and taking a long happy hour that ran well into the evening. He even ate many of his meals with Wally who was as regular as a clock and took his main meal at two o'clock sharp every day. Disdaining cooking since his wife's death four years earlier, Wally always sent Manuel to the restaurant in the hotel next door to pick up its daily special, whatever it happened to be, except, of course, on Wednesdays when he sent Manuel to the Mexican restaurant down the strip for enchiladas, and on Fridays when he dispatched him to pick up Chinese food. One thing Wally never did, in spite of his omnivorous tastes, was actually to go out to eat in any of these restaurants. He had an absolute preference for take-out food. Perhaps this had something to do with his aversion to physical activity, which he confined to his daily ritual of walking to the end of his dock every morning shortly after he got up and stretching his corpulent body. This exhausted him and he always let out a big sigh when he got back on the porch before he collapsed into his lounge chair where, with Ernest in his lap, he spent the rest of the morning drinking coffee and dispensing his wisdom to whoever happened to come by and would listen.

After a week of spending almost every waking hour with Wally, Bob had had enough of inactivity and was eager for something more strenuous. So he asked Wally to make the necessary arrangements to get him out on the turquoise water that looked so enchanting from the vantage point of his hammock on the porch.

With military-like precision, Wally arranged for Bob's introduction to the more active side of island life to begin the next day. In the morning, with the sun shining through wispy white clouds, Gideon pulled up to the dock with a twenty-two-foot-long, open, mahogany boat painted yellow and blue and powered by an old 50-horsepower Mercury outboard. Bob went down to meet him all raring to go, wearing his long swimming trunks, a T-shirt, and a Loganville Country Club golf cap to protect him from the sun.

"Mawnin'," greeted Gideon.

"Where we going today, Gideon?" asked Bob.

"Hol Chan, de marine reserve by de cut in de reef."

Bob stumbled over the snorkeling equipment as he climbed into the boat and took his seat in the bow. The motor roared into action and the boat took off in the direction of the reef. It was only a five-minute ride to their destination. When they got there, Gideon anchored the boat and showed Bob how to put on his mask and snorkel and fins. Gideon told Bob to jump in the water with him and to stick close. There was a big splash as they both hit the water. It was so warm—almost 80 degrees—that there wasn't the shock that Bob expected when he jumped into the water. The water also tasted salty and was much more buoyant than the fresh water in Lake Logan where Bob had done most of his swimming.

Once in the water, Gideon quickly swam up beside Bob. Together, they started out across a flat part of the reef covered with staghorn and mushroom-shaped coral. The water was only about ten feet deep and, since it was low tide, the tops of some of the coral stuck out of the water and looked burned by the sun. The coral forest was separated by flat stretches of white sand and sea grass. As they swam, they could see a large school of yellowtail snapper streaming around a coral outcropping. It was headed for the shade underneath the anchored boat. Once it got there, it took up a position swimming in place into the current. They also saw long, shiny, silver barracudas with sharp teeth gleaming, just floating under the water, looking for their next meal.

When they had gone about eighty feet from the boat, Gideon motioned for Bob to follow him and he executed a perfect surface dive with the bottom half of his body shooting straight up out of the water, which took him right down to the coral head. Bob followed, but with much less style and much more floundering. As they reached the bottom and began to inspect a brain coral, Bob saw with alarm, out of the corner of his eye, a 5-foot nurse shark approaching from behind—not exactly a Great White, but still worrying to someone from the cornfields of central Illinois, whose only exposure to sharks had been in the *Jaws* movies. When the shark got right next to them, Gideon reached out and grabbed it by the tail, quickly flipping it over. Once on its back, the shark wriggled weakly a few times before ceasing its struggle and falling surprisingly dormant. Gideon motioned to Bob to see if he wanted to hold the shark, but he could tell by the way that Bob was quickly backing off that he wanted nothing to do with it. After he was done examining the shark, Gideon turned it upright and let it go. It floated in place for a few seconds taking time to regain its equilibrium and then quickly swam away with two sweeps of its powerful tail. Bob could hardly believe what he was witnessing. He had forgotten for a moment that he was under water and needed to breathe. His lungs nearly bursting, he headed straight up to the surface for air as fast as he could kick. Breaking out of the water, he was filled with excitement and gasping for air.

Gideon surfaced beside Bob and asked, "Yu no lak fish. Jus baby nurse shark. No bite. A no fred a big uns edder."

"It won't bite me if I don't mess with it. That's for sure, Gideon. I don't suppose you ever saw the movie *Jaws*."

"No, nebba see dat."

"Good thing. After I saw it, I was even afraid to take a bath for months."

Gideon signaled for Bob to follow him underwater again. This time he took him down to a small hole in the reef. Looking at Bob, he gave him the biting sign with his hand. Apprehensively, Bob peered closer into the hole and saw a green Moray eel opening and shutting its mouth. Again Bob backed away and headed for the surface.

When they rendezvoused on the surface, Gideon laughed again. "E no bite edder."

They continued to swim along the surface with their snorkels projecting from the water, admiring the multicolored marine life underneath. There were parrot fish, hogfish, and tiny damsel fish, and more schools of yellowtail snapper. As they went past the last outcropping of coral, Bob peered down into the abyss. The wall dropped what looked like a thousand feet to the sea bottom. Bob had a sudden feeling of disorientation and extreme vulnerability. He wondered what frightening sea monsters lay lurking in the dark depth beneath. But all he could see was a giant grouper swimming lazily along below. Bob signaled to Gideon that the time had come to head back to the boat. He was starting to get tired, and, more importantly, he'd had enough for one day.

The swim back to the boat went much faster going with the current. That's the way it's always done so that snorkelers don't go too far from the boat. But still the swim back was enough to really tire Bob out. When they finally reached the boat, they had to climb up the ladder that hung on the back next to the motor. Bob could barely make it, whereas Gideon practically leapt out of the water. Once in the boat, Bob sat on the seat on the side gasping for breath while Gideon cranked up the motor and headed back. After Bob's breathing returned to normal, he leaned back and began to enjoy the warming rays of the sun as the boat cruised homeward. When they reached the dock, Bob saw Wally waiting on the porch and hurried up, anxious to tell him about his adventure.

"Thanks, Wally, for getting Gideon to take me out to the reef. It was an unbelievable experience."

"That's what all my guests tell me. Our barrier reef is always listed as the best and longest in the Western Hemisphere in all of the dive magazines."

"I was blown away when Gideon grabbed a shark and put it to sleep."

"Did he pull that old trick again? He should leave those poor nurse sharks alone. They're harmless, you know."

"Didn't look so harmless to me. Have you ever snorkeled the reef yourself?"

"Oh no! I don't like to go in the water," he said with such vehemence that it startled Ernest the cat who jumped off his lap on to the floor. "I prefer to sit on the porch."

"So I gathered. See you later for lunch," said Bob heading off to his palapa for a nice long snooze to get rested for Wally's twin afternoon rituals of lunch and Happy Hour.

"I'll have Manuel pick you up some jerk chicken and rice and beans from Elvi's Kitchen. It's about time you tried some real Belizean food," said Wally.

"Tell them to go easy on the hot sauce," said Bob.

"Don't worry," said Wally. "It's really pretty bland unless you douse it in Marie Sharpe's fiery hot sauce. That's our favorite down here. Made from habenaro peppers, you know. They make jalapeno peppers taste mild. It will burn your tongue right off."

"You must have not eaten any of it," joked Bob.

Later that night after a few too many piña coladas and not very much hot sauce, Bob went back to his room. For the first time since he'd arrived, he thought about Donna as he lay in bed. He wondered what she was doing. Was it just that he was getting horny? No, it was more than that. He genuinely missed her. While she wasn't perfect, she was all he had. Did he love her? He wasn't sure. After two failed relationships, he wasn't even sure he knew what love was.

Bob felt the need to communicate and reached for the phone even though it was almost midnight. He awkwardly dialed her number in the dark.

"Hello," a sleepy voice answered at the other end of the line.

"Hi, honey, it's me."

"Bob! I was really worried about you. Since I hadn't heard from you in almost two weeks, I thought something must've happened."

"Has it been that long? The time just passes down here. It's very laid back, you know."

"Have you contacted the local Rotary group yet?"

"The what?...Oh, ...no...no, not yet. Maybe next week."

"Well, what have you been doing?" she asked.

"Umm! ...Not much. Today I went snorkeling on the reef. It was like being in one of those undersea nature programs on the Life channel."

"What about you?" he asked. "What are you up to?"

"Oh, the usual—working, renting movies, arguing with Sarah, taking care of Mom. Nothing different really to report."

"Okay, I'd better go. This telephone call is gonna cost me an arm and a leg. It was good to hear your voice."

"I love you, Bob, and miss you."

"Yeah, honey, me too, bye."

Contrary to the pictures in the tourist brochures, every day was not sunny on Ambergrise Caye, expecially in the rainy season, which runs from June to January. One afternoon, as Bob sat on the porch of his palapa, he saw gathering storm clouds in the distance. It looked like a black amorphous mass approaching from beyond the reef. As it got closer, the wind became so strong that it started to toss about the lounge chairs and tables down on the beach as if they were toys. Over at the main building, he could see Wally battening down the shutters. Bob began to do the same. Looking behind him, he saw a solid wall of rain moving off the water and onto the beach. After closing and latching the shutters, Bob retreated inside his palapa to wait out the storm. The wind was so strong that the thatch on the roof fell like confetti on the floor and two lamps were knocked off the tables. The storm finished almost as rapidly as it had come. Bob looked out to see the sun shining again, but branches of palm trees were laying all about and furniture was strewn everywhere.

Later when Bob asked Wally about the storm, he was told not to worry. This was the rainy season. It happened all the time. Only the hurricanes were a problem and there was always plenty of warning. In addition to the usual rain, Bob saw several other real storms while he was on Ambergrise Caye. They always made him marvel at the power of nature and man's vulnerability to the elements. Fishermen scratching out their living on a island only a few feet above sea level must be a hardy breed. He wanted to meet some.

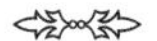

6

Donna had woken up early and was lying in her bed thinking. Bob had been gone for almost a month and he had called only once. Every day she missed him more. It was all the little things they did together: cuddling on the sofa, watching TV, walking around the neighborhood with the dog, and even going shopping. It was having someone to confide in about life's problems: difficulties at work, controversies with Sarah, and parking tickets. Bob may not be the best man in the world, but at least he was hers. Or was he? she wondered. I haven't heard from him for weeks. What the devil was he doing down there anyway in, where was it, that godforsaken place, Belize? Why didn't he call more often? He hadn't taken up with another woman down there, had he? Was he ever going to come back? Doubts gnawed at her like a beaver on a log.

The alarm rang. Seven o'clock, time to get up and get ready for work. She pounded on the wall to wake Sarah up to go to high school. Putting on her robe and her Smurf-blue, furry slippers, she went down to the kitchen to put the coffee pot on. As she shuffled along, she had to be careful not to trip over Toto who always followed her everywhere around the house, constantly staying underfoot.

"What's for breakfast?" asked Sarah, yawning widely.

"You can have whatever type of cereal you like," replied Donna, filling Toto's stainless steel bowl with dried dog food.

"Cereal again. Why not eggs, bacon and toast?"

"You can make it if you want, but I've got to go to the beauty parlor early today. We've got some customers coming in right at nine o'clock and we have to get ready."

"Nah, I'll just have cereal then."

Isn't it amazing how teenagers are so anxious to eat something special until they have to prepare it themselves? thought Donna. And then it's whatever is easiest.

Donna put two bowls, a box of Cheerios and a carton of milk on the table. After pouring herself a cup of coffee, she sat down at the table. She tried to make conversation with Sarah as they both spooned up the yummy little "o"s.

"What are you doing in school today, sweetie?" Donna asked.

"Nothing," Sarah replied.

"Are you gonna come home right after school or are you going somewhere?"

"I dunno."

"When willya know?"

"Later."

"Willya call me at work and let me know?"

"Uh-huh," Sarah sighed. She hated the way her mother was so nosy and always wanted to know where she was going or who she was going to be with, but she didn't feel like arguing this early in the morning.

The silence of an armed truce descended over the room as Donna and Sarah gobbled down their breakfasts, carefully avoiding any eye contact.

Donna was first to finish. She rushed back to the bathroom to take a shower and get ready, leaving Toto still chomping on his food. Sarah huffed. She hated it when she had to wait for her Mom to use the bathroom first.

Donna worked downtown where the buildings were older and the rents lower. She enjoyed the drive downtown on Chicago Street. It was shaded by trees and lined with the stately old turn-of-the-century mansions where the town's elite used to live before they moved out to Loganvale to be near the country club. She preferred the old town to the giant, sterile strip mall complex on Highway 1, Chicago Street's northern extension. It had a certain character. Sure, many of the charming old buildings had become rundown or, worse yet, were boarded up. And the sidewalks were cracked and not all the litter had been picked up. Donna may not have been able to articulate it but this seediness was what gave Loganville its character and made it a real-life place, not just some phony model of small town America like Celebration, which Disney created out of the orange groves near Orlando to cash in on the public's nostalgia for the lost world of Norman Rockwell.

Donna parked her six-year-old Honda Civic with the fuzzy dice hanging from the mirror in the parking lot behind Ellie's Salon and Spa.

She entered the building through the back alley door next to the dumpster. When she got inside, the air conditioner hadn't been turned on yet and the place stank of stale air perfumed with peroxide and hair dyes. Ellie, who was waiting impatiently, pacing back and forth in front of the sink, started in on her before she had even had time to put her purse in the drawer.

"What time did I tell you to come in?" Ellie asked.

"Eight-thirty," Donna replied.

"And what time do you think it is?" she asked, looking angrily at her watch.

"I don't know. I don't have a watch on. You tell me," responded Donna.

"It's twenty till nine," said Ellie. "How can we run a business if you don't get here on time like you're supposed to?"

"Don't worry. We've still got plenty of time to get ready," said Donna.

"I don't care," said Ellie. "I told you to be here at eight-thirty."

"Okay, okay, I'm sorry," said Donna.

The day was very busy. Donna shampooed hair, permed hair, straightened hair, dyed hair, bleached hair. She did everything you could possibly think of to hair, even dry it, a task in which she was assisted by a row of hair dryers that looked like space helmets. All the while she worked, she exchanged small talk and gossip with the many regular customers who had become friends over the years—Mrs. Clinton whose daughter had just had a baby, Julie Smith whose husband owned the local hardware store, Ethel Woods, a retired school teacher who could read the fashion magazines faster than anyone. When lunch time came and the last customer had left, Donna was exhausted and very hungry. She gathered up her purse and started out the door.

"Where do you think you're going? asked Ellie.

"To get a sandwich. I didn't have time this morning to make one," replied Donna.

"You can't just rush off like that. We've still got work to do. I want you to help me hang up some new curtains I bought."

"Can't it wait 'til I get back."

"No, we're too busy this afternoon. We won't have time."

"But I've got to get something to eat."

"You should have made a sandwich."

"But I didn't. I said I'll help you when I get back."

"But I want to do it now. If you walk out of here, don't bother coming back," yelled Ellie.

"Well, if that's the way you feel, I won't," said Donna, letting the door slam shut as she stormed out. I've finally had it with that woman, she huffed to herself as she walked down the street past the old Carnegie Library that had been turned into a War Museum. I'm just not going to put up with that nasty old bitch any more. She's disrespected me for the last time.

Donna continued to walk down the block to the Deluxe Diner. Looking through the front window past the board containing the day's specials, she could see that most of the tables were filled as usual. Only a couple of places remained at the counter. Entering, she waved weakly to a few of the regulars and climbed up on one of the stools at the shiny red counter. She did not really feel much like talking after what had happened, but only wanted to eat. Although she knew the selections by heart, she buried her head in the menu and pretended to study it. A heavy-set, grey-haired waitress with a big smile on her face came over with a coffee pot in her hand.

"Coffee, Donna?" she asked.

"Sure, Phyllis. I could sure use one today."

"What else can I getcha?" Phyllis asked.

"Just a toasted tuna salad sandwich with some coleslaw and a pickle, please," said Donna.

Phyllis reached over and poured some coffee in Donna's cup. Donna picked up her cup and took a sip. It was strong and hot, just the way she liked it. Drinking the coffee, she thought about what had happened and gazed at the cream pies oozing calories in the glass case behind the counter.

"Here's your sandwich, sugar," said Phyllis. "What's wrong? You don't look very happy."

"I had a fight with Ellie and quit," said Donna, barely holding back her tears.

"I'm sorry to hear that," said Phyllis, with the genuine concern of someone who had had a run-in, or two, of her own with bossy employers in the past.

Donna ate her sandwich quietly and drank the rest of her coffee. When she was finished, she got up and went over to the cash register. The owner, Mr. Stilakos, already had her bill ready. She gave him her credit card, and got back the receipt to sign.

Taking a five dollar bill out of her purse and laying it on the counter, she said, "Could you also give me five state lottery tickets for Saturday's draw. My luck has been so bad, I'm due for a change."

After Donna had sulked around the house in her nightgown a couple of days, even Sarah, who like most teenagers, inhabited her own hermetically-sealed, little world and was remarkably oblivious to what was going on in their parents' lives, noticed that her mother was not following her normal routine.

"Got a few days off, Mom?" she finally asked casually, not displaying too much curiosity.

"No, I lost my job," Donna replied listlessly.

"Does that mean we're gonna have to—like—go on welfare?" said Sarah, starting to become more concerned as developments in the adult world threatened to impinge upon her own.

"No, don't worry. I'll find something else before too long," reassured Donna.

"Like what?"

"I don't know. Something."

"I could help. They'd give me another shift at the A&W if I asked. Whaddaya think?"

"No, you already work long enough. You need to concentrate on your schoolwork."

"Oh! Mom, you always say that. School is such a drag."

"No, you worry about school. Let me worry about paying the bills."

"Ah, Mom!"

"Tonight, I think I'm gonna go to my aerobics class. It will do me good to get out of the house. And then maybe Connie and I will go out afterwards."

"That'll be good," said Sarah, seeing an opportunity and starting to think that maybe she'd take advantage of her mother's absence to throw a little party.

Down in the basement of the Calvary Baptist Church, all the chairs and tables were stacked neatly by the wall and the light green tile floor was clear of obstructions. Dressed in black tights and one of Bob's extra large Eastern Illinois University T-shirts, Donna stood in a line next to her redheaded friend Connie. In front stood Cathy Hill, their bouncing blond aerobics instructor, wearing sleek purple lycra tights and a matching sports bra. Cathy's flat athletic tummy adorned with a gold belly-button ring was the envy of the other women who like Donna and

Connie averaged ten to twenty years older and were more shy about revealing their less-than-perfectly-toned midriffs.

Before they started in, Cathy announced, "I heard from Joanne yesterday. She had her baby on Monday. It was a boy—eight pounds three ounces. The mother and baby are doing fine."

Everyone cheered loudly.

"Are we gonna send her a baby present?" said Kelly, the member of the group who had most recently had a baby herself and felt a special responsibility to continue the tradition.

"What do you think, girls?" asked Cathy.

A chorus of approvals rang out.

"Okay, who wants to volunteer to collect the money and buy the present?" said Cathy.

"I'd be glad to do it," answered Kelly.

"Okay, now that that's settled, let's get down to work," said Cathy, reaching over to turn on the ghetto blaster.

Brittany Speer's voice singing "Baby One More Time," blared from the speakers.

"Okay, girls, let's get warmed up," said Cathy. "March in place."

"Now, grapevine left. Hamstring, repeat, four, three, two, one."

"Abduct, repeat, four, three, two, one."

"Heel, dig, repeat, four, three, two, one."

"Ski, repeat, four, three, two, one."

"Okay, harder. Lunge, repeat, four, three, two, one."

"Now let's do some stretches, follow me."

"Okay, knee up, with bounce, high, repeat, four, three, two, one."

Now, squats, squeeze those glutes, repeat, four, three, two, one."

"V-step, four, three, two, one, repeat, four, three, two, one."

"Straddle jumps, repeat, four, three, two, one."

Stopping only occasionally to allow everyone to catch their breath and guzzle water, Cathy continued to cycle through the exercises with military precision as one song followed another from the mix playing on the boom box. By the end of the scheduled hour, Donna had worked up a real sweat.

"Okay, girls, time for the cool-down. March in place."

Donna was glad to hear those words. She was really bushed, but she knew she had enough left in her to make it through the final few minutes. It wasn't long before she heard the welcome voice of Cathy announcing, "Okay, girls, that's it for this week."

Breathing heavily, Donna went over to one of the tables and picked up her towel to wipe off her forehead. Connie came over and joined her.

"That calls for some refreshment," said Connie, her green eyes sparkling. "You want to go up to Gallagher's."

"Sure, just let me get cleaned up and change."

They both picked up their sports bags and headed off for the restroom that also served as a dressing room. After they had changed, they exchanged good-byes and hugs with Cathy and the other women who through several years of shared suffering had become their friends.

Gallagher's Road House on the highway north of town was the local honky tonk. When Donna and Connie got there, it was really hopping even for a Wednesday night. Two men in jeans and cowboy boots—one with a mustache and a black hat and the other with sideburns and a goatee—were doing a pretty good job of impersonating Kix Brooks and Ronnie Dunn singing "Rock My World." At the appropriate point in the song, the crowd would join in and bellow out "Little Country Girl." The dance floor in front of the band was filled, and it was standing room only at the bar. In their tight jeans and boots, Donna and Connie looked right at home as they boogied their way across the floor to a free booth in the far corner, and slid in.

"Have you heard from Bob?" Connie asked.

"Yeah, once," replied Donna.

"Only once! What did he say?"

"Not much, said he'd been snorkeling."

"Snorkeling? That's all he said after all this time? That he'd been snorkeling? Whaddaya think he's up to down there?"

"I don't know."

"I'll bet he's cheating on you for sure. With a man like him you might as well not have one. As soon as they get out of your sight, they act as if they're free as birds. You know I speak from experience. I've gone out with too many of his type."

Just then a waitress passed with a tray of draft above her head. "Hey ma'am, can we get a couple of beers over here? We're dying of thirst," Connie shouted.

"I don't think he's like that at all," said Donna, looking slightly worried by Connie's remarks.

"Yes, he is. You ought to dump him and find a new man while you still can," Connie said. "We're not getting any younger, you know."

"But I like him. I feel comfortable being around him."

"I feel the same about my old shoes, but that doesn't mean I wouldn't swap them for a shiny new pair if I had the chance."

"I don't know. He makes me laugh. And he can still turn me on. Maybe I...uh... even love him."

"Plee...ease, you're not a school girl any more who can afford to be moping around in love. You've got your future to think about. And Sarah's, too. Speaking about the future, have you started looking for a new job yet?"

"No, I haven't much felt like it."

They were interrupted by two men coming up to their table: one was tall and dark, the other blond with a mustache and average height. Both looked right at home in their jeans and western shirts.

"Excuse me, ladies, can we interest you in a dance?" asked the tall dark one.

"No, thanks," said Donna. "I really don't feel like it."

"Oh, come on," said Connie. "We don't want to disappoint these handsome gentlemen. And besides I really want to dance. Let's have some fun for a change."

"Okay, if you say so, but just one dance."

The tall one took Donna by the hand out to the dance floor where they were doing the Texas two-step. The other grabbed Connie. It wasn't long before Donna was really enjoying the dancing. Her partner sure knew how to dance and moved very fluidly. For the next song, the Brooks and Dunn impersonators started to play the "Boot Scootin' Boogie." Dancers quickly formed up into three lines. Donna liked the way line dancing was choreographed. Swivel, swivel, left... Touch right toe forward... Shuffle, shuffle, right... Slap right foot behind... Kick...Stomp. It required much more concentration than the free moving rock and roll dancing she had learned as a young girl. She was glad to be dancing in time with everyone else. It made her feel good. Why couldn't she get Bob to go line dancing sometime? she thought. It would be such fun!

After the dance was over, the tall man asked, "Would you like to join us for a drink?"

"No, sorry, I have to get home and check on my daughter," said Donna.

She went back to the table. Connie followed.

"You're sure a party pooper," Connie said. "I thought they were kinda cute."

"I'm not ready for this," said Donna, suddenly becoming moody and morose. "Let's go home."

On their way out, there was a sign on the wall. "Waitresses wanted, Full- or Part-Time."

"That one's got your name on it," said Connie, recalling how she and Donna had worked together as waitresses in a bar for a few years after they graduated from high school and before they both got married.

"Yeah," said Donna. "I should give them a call tomorrow."

There was a big Harley-Davidson Hog parked in front of her house when Donna got home. Inside she found a motorcycle jacket hanging from the hook in the hall. It was emblazoned with "Hell's Riders" and had a crest with a devil riding a motorcycle on the back. Steeling herself for what she feared she was going to find, she continued into the recreation room. There sat a strange man in a sleeveless T-shirt with his hairy tattooed arm around her darling, innocent Sarah who, in her eyes, was still a little girl in spite of her ample endowments. They were smoking marijuana and watching television.

"Mother!" said Sarah, looking up with surprise.

"What are you two doing?"

"Just watching TV."

"You think I'm so dumb I don't know what marijuana smells like? YOU, whoever you are, get the hell out of here. And YOU, young lady, we're going to have a serious talk."

Donna stood waiting while Sarah's bandanna-wearing friend sullenly got up off the couch.

"You better go, Joe," said Sarah. "I'll call you tomorrow."

He sighed and rolled his eyes as if to say to Sarah, how can you put up with this crap from this old bitch. Then he turned and stomped out the door, his shit-kicker motorcycle boots clicking on the hall floor as he left.

"Well, what do you have to say for yourself?" asked Donna.

"I was just trying the marijuana. Joe had a little."

"I'll bet he did!"

"It was my first time, Mom. Didn't you ever try it."

"Er...we're talking about you here, not me. Don't you know that marijuana is addictive? That it can lead to more dangerous drugs? That it can even cause people to become schizophrenic?"

"People just say that to scare us kids. It's no big deal for me."

"Well, it's a big deal for me. It's illegal. And as long as you live in this house, you live by my rules and I don't want you smoking it. And I don't want you seeing that motorcycle guy, whoever he is."

"Yeah, yeah, yeah," Sarah said. "Can I go now?"

"Yes, you can go right up to bed. Remember you have to get up early tomorrow and go to school."

When Sarah left, Donna felt drained. She collapsed on the couch. What can I do? she asked herself. It's sure hard trying to raise a teenager all by yourself. There's so much more trouble they can get in nowadays.

7

Several days later, a few blocks away from Loganville High School, Sarah's friend Joe was standing by his motorcycle in an alley next to a derelict industrial building. He was talking to two teenage boys named Tom and Bill who had just pulled up in a white Pontiac Sunfire convertible. The boys, both juniors at the high school, looked like typical teenagers. With baseball hats on their heads, they wore loose-fitting, short-sleeve shirts over T-shirts, their baggy pants hung down low around their asses and almost covered their expensive running shoes.

"I can give you a deal," Joe said. "I'll only charge you twenty dollars for two of these papers. They each contain two hits. You know regularly I'd charge twice as much. What do you say?"

"I dunno," Tom said.

"What's the matter, you afraid of a little crack?" Joe smirked.

"No," said Tom, not wanting to look timid in front of his friend.

"Then you'll take some?" said Joe.

"Uh-huh," said Tom.

Later that night, Tom was at a party in a Federalist-style house over on Elmwood Drive in a well-to-do neighborhood near the municipal golf course. The parents of the teenager who lived there were out of town and word had somehow gotten out all over town about a big party. Almost a hundred people were already there, most of them juniors and seniors at Loganville High School. The kitchen of the house was filled with coolers of ice, cases of beer and pop, and an assortment of bottles of rum, vodka and rye. The drinking was pretty heavy and many of the young people were already feeling their booze and starting to get a little rowdy. One boy had already knocked a lamp off one of the tables and another had spilled a drink on the oriental rug in the living room. The boy whose parents owned the house was starting to panic and was running around asking everyone to please leave, but nobody was paying much attention to his pathetically inept efforts. As far as they were concerned, if he hadn't wanted a party, he shouldn't have told anyone his parents weren't home and to come on over.

In the library off the living room, Tom was standing in a circle with a girl he liked named Pam and a few other couples. He had already drunk two beers and three large glasses of rum and coke and was feeling no pain. With the alcohol reducing his inhibitions, he took one of the folded papers out of his pocket.

"Look what I got," he slurred.

"What is it?" asked another boy named Dick.

"It's crack," Tom said.

"What do you do with it?" Don asked.

"You smoke it," Tom said. "Don't you know anything?"

"Well, there's a pipe here on the desk. Why don't you show us how it's done."

"Okay," said Tom.

"You better not, Tom," warned Pam.

"Don't worry," said Tom. "I can handle it."

Tom filled the pipe with the crack cocaine from one of the folded papers. Tom took the first puff and passed the pipe to Don who took another. The boys passed the pipe back and forth becoming increasingly euphoric the more they inhaled. Tom took the biggest drags. When they were done with the first envelope, Tom fumbled in his pocket for the second. This time it was only him smoking the rest of the crack. Don declined to smoke any more. He'd had enough.

As Tom smoked more, he became increasingly hyper, talking up a storm about nothing in particular that made any sense. After a while, he began to shake a bit and wobble on his feet. He looked very pale. Pam started to become alarmed. The next thing she knew Tom keeled right over on the floor.

She rushed over to see what was the matter.

"Oh my God, oh my God," she screamed when she leaned down next to him. "He's not breathing. Somebody call 911."

The festive atmosphere of the party suddenly turned very somber as a large crowd of teenagers in various states of inebriation stood solemnly around staring at Tom laying on the floor, while they helplessly waited for the rescue squad to arrive.

In less than ten minutes, two husky black men with a stretcher arrived and pushed their way through the crowd. They lifted Tom's inert body on top and carried him out to the ambulance.

When Tom arrived at the Loganville Hospital, the Pakistani doctor working in the Emergency Room pronounced Tom DOA. The subsequent autopsy determined that the cause of death was an excess in the bloodstream of cocaethylene, a substance produced in the human liver by the combination of alcohol and cocaine. It intensifies cocaine's effect and is a common cause of death among those who mix alcohol and cocaine.

Another naive and foolish teenager had fallen victim to drug abuse. His death would be the talk of the town for a week or two before it was forgotten. This happens all too often. There is an unstoppable river of cocaine flowing into the United States from South America through Central America and the Caribbean destroying lives and corrupting governments.

8

Bob woke up at dawn filled with anticipation. It was the day he was going to go marlin fishing. This was quite a step up from catching crappies in the Green Fork River below the Lake Logan dam. He had to get ready quickly. Gideon would soon be at the dock to pick him up to take him to the wharf where the charter boat was docked. Bob put on his T-shirt, swimming trunks and tennis shoes as quickly as he could and rushed down to the dock. The sun rising above the turquoise Caribbean was blinding. Shading his eyes, he looked out and saw Gideon's boat coming in the distance. When Gideon pulled up alongside the dock, Bob hopped in.

"Hi, Gideon, I'm really excited to be going out fishing. It looks like we're going to have a perfect day for it," said Bob.

"Yeah, maan." said Gideon, as he headed the boat up island.

As they approached the center of the town where the wharves were located, they saw the *Mary Dee* moored to the pier. She was a twenty-nine-foot Topaz Sportfisher fully equipped with a tower and a Lee fighting chair with a bucket and harness in the back. And was she ever sleek and beautiful! Worth every penny to Bob of the four hundred dollars it was going to cost him to charter her for the day.

"Hey, maan!" said Gideon to the plump mestizo captain who welcomed Bob and Gideon aboard.

"Bienvenidos, señores," he responded. "I am Juan Salazar at your service. Permit me to introduce you to my crew Pablo and Ricardo."

"Glad to meet you," said Bob, shaking hands all around. "I'm really looking forward to today. Are the marlin biting?" he asked the Captain eagerly.

"Mas o menos, señor, it's a very tricky business. There aren't many marlins these days. Overfishing, you know. Catching one involves either many days fishing or plain luck."

Bob gulped, thinking that, with his money running out, he couldn't afford to go out any more days fishing at four hundred dollars a pop. He would have to rely on luck, which for him recently hadn't been all that good.

The crew busied themselves loading up the day's provisions and arranging the equipment. They also filled up the bait well with small mackerel and mullets. Captain Juan went up front to look at some charts and plan the day's voyage. In about a quarter of an hour they were ready to shove off. The *Mary Dee* backed off the dock and then set course for the cut in the reef at one-quarter throttle so as not to create a big wake. In ten minutes they were through the cut. The Captain then opened the boat up and she soon reached her cruising speed of twenty-one knots. After a half-hour, the boat slowed down and Captain Juan turned the wheel over to Pablo and told Ricardo to get the equipment ready. He came to the stern where Bob was sitting with Gideon to begin the briefing on the ABCs of marlin fishing that he gave to all the wannabe Hemingways of the world who made up most of his clientele.

Ricardo brought back a rod and reel to Captain Juan. More precisely for the aficionados, it was a 6/0 reel loaded with 50 pound test Dacron line mounted on a graphite rod. At the end of the line was a 12 foot Sevalon leader of 80-pound test and a 9/0 hook. The captain showed Bob the proper way to sit in the fighting chair and how to keep the rod in the gimble, which means to insert the end of rod in the pivoting holder on the front of the chair to facilitate playing the fish. He also gave Bob a quick course in the basics of marlin fishing. Afterwards Bob sat in the chair, nervously fiddling with the rod and reel and wondering if he would be up to the challenge, conveniently forgetting that most likely he wouldn't be lucky enough even to face a challenge.

After more than an hour of cruising around, an excited cry rang out from the tower. It was Pablo. "¡Hay uno alli! ¡Hay uno alli!"

Jumping up out of the chair, Bob asked excitedly, "What did he say?"

"E say dere's a fockin' big fish over der, maan," translated Gideon from one foreign tongue to another, albeit one that Bob was beginning to understand. "E can see de fin stickin' out of de water. See over der unter de laughin' gulls."

"By God, he's right! I can see something thrashing around in the water under the sea gulls. The fish must be feeding."

Pablo steered the boat in the direction of the bubbling water, and began to circle. Ricardo took another rod and cast out behind the boat. On the end of the line was a foot-long highly-colored teaser lure without hooks. Once it got out far enough, he stuck the rod in one of the holders and began to bait Bob's line. He took a ten-inch-long mullet and harnessed it so that it would ski on the surface of the water behind the boat without twisting. He then set Bob's reel in freewheeling with the clicker on and the star drag set with enough tension to fight the fish without breaking the line. When he was finished, he nodded and Bob began to let the line out behind the boat. The captain circled around again, bringing Bob's line directly in front of the great fish.

"He's going for the bait," Captain Juan shouted as the fish dived. "Let me know when you can feel him on the line. Then I'll have Pablo start to take up slack. Wait till you can count to twenty to give him time to swallow the hook before setting it."

"He's taken the bait!" yelled Bob excitedly. The line sliced the water running away from the tip of the pole. The boat plunged ahead, further tightening the line. After what seemed like an eternity, but really wasn't even the full twenty seconds the Captain had told him to wait, the line was finally taut. Bob jerked on the pole for all he was worth. It bent over double and the reel whirred as the line flew out. The hook was definitely set. The fish had the strength of a lassoed bull.

"Reel and pump the rod rhythmically," shouted the Captain. "It will make the fish jump and wear himself out."

As instructed, Bob alternately reeled and pumped, and then reeled and pumped some more. Finally, the great blue fish jumped out of the water. Then, just as quickly, he sounded, going straight for the bottom. Pablo maneuvered the boat forward, keeping the line taut and always at an angle. The battle raged on for the better part of an hour with many more jumps and dives. Bob felt like his arms were going to fall off. Worried that his arms would cramp up, he didn't know if he'd be able to hold on long enough to boat his long-billed adversary. Anyway, he called on reserves of endurance he didn't know he had and fought on for another quarter hour as the fish gradually wore himself out, each jump getting weaker and each dive shallower.

"I don't hate the great fish," said Bob wearily. "He is my brother and I love him, but he has to die."

"Otro lleno de ideas mierdas de Hemingway," the Captain whispered to Ricardo.

After an hour and a half of struggle, Bob finally managed to work the fish right up next to the dive deck where he rested motionless under only one foot of water. The Captain, who had been standing behind the chair all the time patiently waiting, saw that the fight was over. He nodded to

Ricardo who was standing next to him with a gaff hook in hand. Leaning over the back of the boat, Ricardo hooked the huge fish in the mouth and gill. Gideon saw Ricardo struggling and grabbed another gaff hook and hooked it into the other side of the mouth. Together the two men managed to hoist the fish on board. Then they all stood around admiring their giant blue catch.

"He's a real prize," Captain Juan said. "He must weigh over three hundred pounds. That's pretty big for a blue marlin. We don't catch many like this around here anymore."

"Yu got dere wan hell of a fish, maan!" said Gideon. "We all be a eatin' him fur a month."

"Now I know why Ernest Hemingway loved marlin fishing so much," said Bob, waxing philosophical and confirming the Captain's diagnosis. "I feel like I've tested my strength against the forces of nature and come out on top."

The great blue fish flipped his tail one last time. Pablo stilled him with a crushing blow on his head. Bob winced at the thud. There was something obscene about killing such a magnificent animal. But it had to be done. It was what fishing was all about. These were real fishermen he was with, not the namby-pamby catch and release types found in Florida.

Bob held on to the railing on the way back as the *Mary Dee* raced smoothly over the waves. Enjoying the feeling of the wind and the sun on his aching muscles, he waved magnanimously to the lobster fishermen whose mahogany sailboats were anchored to the reef. Every once in a while he shot a glance at the splendid blue body of his catch lying inert on the deck, feeling both pride and guilt.

When their boat pulled up alongside the pier, they were greeted with shouts of approval from the other fishermen who were already back and still standing around exchanging fish stories. The cheers got louder as the crew attached the prize marlin to a hoist and hung him up for display on the crossbar at the end of the pier. Bob felt very proud standing next to the mighty blue fish as he accepted the accolades of the growing crowd of fishermen that seemed to be materializing from nowhere, attracted by the prospect of seeing what was apparently becoming an increasingly rare sight. It would be the cause for a big celebration tonight at the local fishermen's bar, which Bob wasn't going to miss even if it did end up costing him a few rounds of drinks.

Around sunset, Bob headed up towards town, treading the well-worn path along the shoreline. The palm trees behind the hotels shaded the narrow strip of sand that dropped off at the end of properties littered with beach furniture and hammocks, docks and rocks. Miami Beach it was not, but it had a small-scale, lived-in type of charm all its own.

Bob was on his way to meet Gideon and Captain Juan at the Tackle Box Bar for a few celebratory beers. Bob had tried to convince Wally to come along, but he had declined, saying that he had enough beer where he was and didn't need to go anywhere else to get more. The Tackle Box Bar was a ramshackle unpainted shack, built on the end of a dock. Below it was a fenced off corral containing eight sharks. To facilitate viewing, a ten foot square hole had been cut out of the floor. To comply with the rigorous local safety standards, a two foot railing had been built around the hole. It was just about right to catch you by the shins if you weren't looking and to give you that very special close-up view of the scary, giant black shapes swimming below.

Bob went out on the dock and into the shack. It was filled with twenty or so grizzled Belizeans who looked like fishermen, and a handful of tourists who stuck out in their colorful vacation attire. As soon as he entered, people began clapping. Apparently, his fame had preceded him. Bob smiled and acknowledged the tribute by looking around and tipping his cap. For the first time in his life, he had apparently done something noteworthy and was getting some recognition. It felt good. Walking carefully around the hole, he stopped to take a peek at a twelve- foot-long shark below before joining the Captain and Gideon at the table.

"De great backra fishaman fu come," ribbed Gideon good-naturedly. "Drink fu all a we," he yelled at the waiter motioning all around the bar with his hand.

For just an instant, Bob had some doubts about the authenticity of his new-found celebrity status. Maybe they're only cheering for the free drinks, he thought. Then he was overwhelmed by another round of applause. What the hell! he said to himself. If I'm giving a party in my honor I might as well enjoy it. Besides it's too late to weasel out.

Captain Juan was more restrained and courtly in his greeting, "Buenas noches, Señor Wayne," he said politely, rising slightly from his chair and touching his cap.

Bob consumed one beer after another while he relived the day's great triumph, getting more and more into the swing of things. The Captain and he, alternating between English and Spanish with a healthy dose of Spanglish thrown in for good measure, told and retold the story of the day's catch to an appreciative audience well lubricated with several rounds of free drinks. Each time, encouraged by hearty cheers, the story got more heroic until it eclipsed Santiago's three-day struggle with the marlin, almost rivaling Captain Ahab's epic battle with Moby Dick.

Finally, Bob reached the saturation point and got up to heed nature's call. He was already beginning to stagger. To be on the safe side, he kept one hand on the wall and navigated well around the gaping hole in the floor. Returning to the table by the same circuitous route, he ordered up another beer. It was a Belikan that the waiter brought and put on the table. Staring at the bottle in front of him through an alcohol-induced haze, he saw something for the first time. It was Belize's famous jade head, which was displayed prominently on the label and stared back at him.

After he had consumed that final bottle of beer, Bob realized that if he didn't leave soon, somebody was going to have to carry him back to Wally's even if he was the world's greatest fisherman. But first he had to pay the tab for all the rounds of beers he had stood, which would take a good chunk of his rapidly dwindling money. Standing up and reaching into his pocket, he pulled his wallet out. Then the drink finally caught up with him and he stumbled towards the center of the room. Catching himself on the miniature railing just in the nick of time to avoid tumbling in, he let his wallet slip out of his hand and fall into the big hole in the floor where, after landing in the water, it fluttered gracefully to the bottom like a butterfly.

"What am I gonna do now?" moaned Bob. "It's got all my money in it and my credit cards to boot."

"Why don't you call American Express?" joked someone who even in Belize had seen the ubiquitous advertisement. The crowd roared with laughter.

As Bob stood staring disconsolately down into the large hole. His white knight emerged at his side in the form of Gideon. "No problem, maan," he said. And to everyone's astonishment, he leapt over the railing like a leopard, barely missing a giant shark that was snoozing in the middle of the hole. The beast was so startled by the totally unexpected splash that it gave one powerful stroke of its huge tail and shot like a lightning bolt to the farthest corner of the pen where it cowered like a kicked dog. The other slightly less astonished sharks also gave Gideon as wide a berth as possible. This left him standing alone in water that was only three feet deep. He was consequently able to lean over and pick up the wallet without even getting his dreadlocks wet. He then waded over to the wall and scampered up. The bar burst into wild applause. Grinning from ear to ear, Gideon ceremoniously presented Bob with the soggy wallet and then turned and bowed to the cheering crowd. He knew that he had done something that night that would go down in island lore, surpassing perhaps even the exploits of the great backra fisherman from Illinois. It was much more important than the paper and plastic in the wallet. It was his own little piece of immortality.

Bob didn't know what to say to his wild and crazy friend other than "Thank you, Gideon." He truly was grateful to get his wallet back and didn't mind sharing his glory. Moreover, heroic fisherman or not, there was no way he would have gone in the water to get it himself—cowardice or good sense, call it what you will. He looked in the wallet to make sure everything was still there. Not so much money left, he thought, but at least he still had his credit cards. Thank God for plastic, he thought.

9

Several days later when he finally got over his colossal hangover from his night of triumphant excess, Bob got up early in the morning and joined a group of six other tourists on one of Wally's suggested day trips from San Pedro. The group, made up of a retired couple, a pair of young honeymooners, and two young women backpackers, took a boat across to the mainland and up the Northern River to Maskall where they transferred to a van that conveyed them up the Old Northern Highway to the Tower Bridge outside of the town of Orange Walk. There they boarded a boat captained by a man in his late twenties named Fernando. He wore a bandanna on his head that made him look more like a pirate than an "eco-tourism guide." But who could deny that was exactly what it said on his T-shirt above a multicolored image of a toucan or beakbird as it was fittingly called in Belize.

It wasn't long before Bob and his new friends were speeding up the New River on an expedition to Lamanai, which means "Submerged Crocodile" in the Mayan language. This was a Mayan site buried deep in the jungle on the New River Lagoon. The trip up the river was the closest that anyone in the group would probably ever want to come to an adventure, a real-life Indiana Jones fantasy. Even though the river wound its way through the thick vegetation and became very narrow in spots with branches overhanging the boat, Fernando delighted in keeping the throttle of the Yamaha eighty-horsepower engine wide open, fishtailing around all the turns, for an extra thrilling effect. Startled crocodiles and turtles jumped into the water at the sound of the approaching vessel and water birds of all sizes and colors took to the air in a panic. The roar of the engine even woke up a colony of rare fish-eating bats sleeping in a hollow tree. In a flutter of activity, they took off in every which direction seeking to escape. It was hard to get a good look at any of the abundant wildlife that lived along the river going at such a break-neck speed. But this was all part of the exciting real-life adventure they were paying for. The eco-tourism would have to wait.

When the river widened out at the mouth to the lagoon and the boat's course became straighter and steadier, the older man finally felt secure enough to relax his hold on the gunwale and reached for his pack. After some searching around, he pulled out a pair of binoculars and a book. Then he began to look around with the binoculars. Seeing something in the distance, he became very excited and began consulting the book frantically until he found what he was looking for.

"Look over there wading along by the shore. It's a jabiru stork!"

And sure enough, there it was—a white, long-legged bird standing about four feet tall and with a wingspan of eight feet.

"You know, the jabiru is Belize's largest bird," he announced, evidently getting this bit of trivia from his bird guide book.

The man, who was wearing a many-pocketed vest over a khaki outfit and looking every bit the bird-watcher he was, passed around his binoculars so that everyone could have a look. A little later, he identified another large, long-necked, brownish bird sitting on a tree branch with its wings extended.

"There's a cormorant over there drying out its wings. Its feathers get waterlogged when it dives for fish. It can only fly again after drying itself out in the sun," he said.

As they went by a group of solidly-constructed wooden houses on the shore, Bob saw another boat containing four white men all dressed alike in straw hats and overalls, heading for a dock. They were carrying a load of uncut lumber, perhaps taking it back to the building he saw on the shore behind the palm trees that looked like some kind of mill. Bob was surprised to see such a group on the river. He wondered who they were and how they had come to live in the middle of the jungle.

After another ten or fifteen minutes of heading up the center of the lagoon, the boat veered westward and headed for the shore. As they approached closer, they could see that what appeared to be a hill from a distance was actually an overgrown and eroded limestone Mayan pyramid, towering more than a hundred feet over a large plaza. What they didn't know was that when this temple was built, it was the tallest structure in the Mayan world and was designed to impress everyone with the great power and wealth of the city's rulers. But from their reaction, it was clear that it retained its capacity to inspire awe after almost two thousand years or five baktuns as the four-hundred-year periods in which the Maya divided time were called.

Fernando adroitly reversed the throttle as he came up to the dock. The boat slowed abruptly and bumped gently against the buoys. After everyone was assembled on the shore near the dock, Fernando transformed himself from the maniacal boat racer into the cordial tour guide. While he passed out box lunches of rice and beans and roast chicken, Belize's national dish, he informed everyone that the tour would start in a half-hour and that if they went off on their own they should be back at the boat by three o'clock sharp, not Belize time, he stressed, or they might find themselves permanently residing in the jungle.

Bob took his box lunch and retreated to a picnic table where he was joined by the retired couple. He gobbled down his food while they debated the appropriate nomenclature of the various different types of multicolored birds flying all about. Suddenly, the woman became very agitated. She had noticed some round holes in the ground surrounding the table and was afraid that there may be snakes in them. Her husband called Fernando over to find out.

"There aren't snakes in those holes, are there?" he asked.

"No, Señor, certainly not serpents."

"What's in them, then?"

"I show you," Fernando said, reaching down on the ground to pluck a long piece of grass with a seed cluster at the end. Clearing his throat, he spit on the seed cluster and stuck the piece of grass down the hole. When he pulled it up, a huge, black, furry tarantula as big as a mouse was hanging on the end.

The woman screamed and grabbed her husband's arm. "Sometimes it's best not to ask too many questions," the husband said, patting her on the shoulder.

At this point, Bob lost his appetite. He excused himself to seek out a Canadian archeologist from the Royal Ontario Museum working at the site with whom Wally had arranged a private tour. He was supposed to meet Wally's friend at the small museum not far from the landing. It shouldn't be hard to find, he thought.

Bob walked over to the small structure nearby. It was dark and smoky inside when he peered in through the open door. Sitting on a chair inspecting a large Mayan bowl was the distinguished archeologist himself, Dr. Simon Butterfield. When he heard Bob, he looked up over his rimless glasses, which were riding low on his nose, and exhaled a cloud of smoke from his pipe.

"You must be Bob Wayne," he said, putting the bowl down on a table covered in artifacts. "Wally told me to expect you. How's he doing, by the way? I haven't seen the old reprobate yet on this trip. I usually spend a week or so with him on San Pedro to relax when I'm down."

"Oh, Wally's the same."

"He sure loved to talk about the Mayans. He's read almost everything written about them, you know. But as much as I've tried, I could never get him to come up here."

"I'm not surprised."

"You interested in Mayan archeology?"

"A bit. Wally told me that as long as I was down here I just had to come up here and see this site. He said it was something I shouldn't miss. And so far he's been right. The main pyramid is really spectacular the way it stands out above the jungle."

"Let me show you around some more," said Dr. Butterfield, getting out of his chair. He was an ordinary-looking man of middle age wearing jeans and a work shirt, but he had a certain sparkle in his eyes that revealed a keen interest in the world around him. "We'll start at N10-43."

Bob wasn't sure exactly what this technical gobbledegook meant, but he dutifully followed Dr. Butterfield over towards the base of the massive main temple anyway, expecting that its meaning would be revealed to him in due course. On their way, they took a meandering path that passed by a smaller pyramid with a giant limestone face. It was twice as high as a man and was carved on one side of the stairway and covered by a ramshackle roof.

"That face is characteristically classic Mayan," said Dr. Butterfield, stopping to admire it intently. "See the elongated forehead. The Mayan aristocrats used to flatten their babies' skulls with boards. The bared teeth between the thick lips was supposed to frighten enemies. That head is one of a matched set. There's another one on the other side that we haven't dug up yet. We don't want to expose it to the elements any sooner than necessary."

Then Dr. Butterfield motioned for Bob to continue to follow him. Soon they reached the base of the main pyramid. It too was made of limestone, but much of the front was crumbling. Only the stairs in the center going all the way up to the summit were reasonably intact. The back which had yet to be excavated still had trees growing on it.

"This is it, N10-43—the largest Pre-classic structure in all of the Mayan world. It's 112 feet tall. Let's climb to the top. From there, you can see the whole site and all the surrounding countryside."

"Wait a minute," said Bob, standing at the base looking up with wonderment and some trepidation as Dr. Butterfield started to climb the steep steps.

When the archeologist had gone up about twenty steps, he turned to look for Bob. Seeing him still at the bottom, he shouted, "Come on. It's not as steep as it looks." That was all the prodding Bob needed, and he started the arduous climb. By the time they reached the top, both of the out-of-shape, middle-aged men were breathing heavily.

"That wasn't so bad. Was it?" huffed Dr. Butterfield.

"It's not the going up I was worried about but the going down," said Bob, looking down the steep steps nervously.

"I've been up here hundreds of times, but I still feel the same feeling of wonder that I experienced twenty years ago as a young graduate student on my first dig. This may not be the tallest Mayan structure in Belize—those at Caracol and Xunantinich are higher—but you have to admit that the view is hard to beat. It's so flat all around you can see forever. Look over there across the New River Lagoon. See the jungle canopy all around below us? It's made up of trees like guancastes, mahogany, and cohune palms and hides many other Mayan structures—more than 700 by my reckoning. This site covers a square mile. At its peak, thirty-five thousand Maya lived here. In fact, this site may be the longest inhabited Mayan city. It was first settled some three thousand years ago and flowered in the Pre-classic period around 100 A.D. when the largest temples were built. And it continued to flourish through the Classic period, which ran from 300 A.D. to 900 A.D. Even when the Spanish conquistadors arrived in the sixteenth century, it was still inhabited, although its population had declined precipitously and its temples had fallen into disrepair. But even so, there were still enough people here for the Spanish to build a church. Look over there to the south along the lagoon, you can still see its ruins."

"What caused the collapse of Mayan civilization?" asked Bob.

"Whew! That's the million dollar question for archeologists specializing in Mesoamerica. I've been studying it all my adult life and I'm afraid I still don't know the complete answer. Possible causes that have been advanced include plague, drought, soil exhaustion, internecine warfare and the associated ritual sacrifice, and peasant revolt. Probably they all played some role, but to what extent we really don't know for sure. The only thing that is clear is that no stelae or stone pillars have been found dating after the tenth century which marked the end of the Classical period. In addition, the skeletons that we uncovered decreased in size over the Classical period, indicating that the peasantry became increasingly stunted by malnutrition, which would be consistent with drought or soil exhaustion due to overpopulation. One strange thing that gives me the creeps, even though I'm a scientist and don't believe in native superstitions, is that the disastrous decline in Mayan civilization occurred after 830 B.C., which marked the start of the tenth baktun as the Mayan measured time in their four-hundred-year Long Count. In their iconography, ten was represented by Lahun, the death lord with a fleshless jaw, who was believed to preside over the tenth baktun. Fear was consequently widespread in the Mayan world that it would be a period of cosmic cataclysm. Eerie, isn't it? It could have been a self-fulfilling prophecy. But enough speculation for now. Are you ready to go down and see some of the sites up close?"

"Okay, but it was easier for me going up," said Bob, nervously turning to go down the steps crawling backward like a crawdad, using his hands as well as his feet.

When they finally reached the bottom, Dr. Butterfield said, "You can stand up and turn around now. We're on the ground again." Only then did Bob feel safe enough to resume his normal bipedal gait.

"In front of the pyramid here is a small ball court where the Mayan played their game of *pok-ta-pok.* The game was pretty simple, although rules varied from one place to another. It was played with a rubber ball. There were two sides. Players were only allowed to hit the ball with their hips or knees. The object of the game was to get the ball through that hoop over there. Sometimes the winners were rewarded with the property of spectators. Other times the losers were put to death. The game was connected to the Mayan creation myth as set out in the *Popul Vuh.* According to this, their holy book, the Mayan ancestral twins defeated the Lords of Death on a ball court."

"Doesn't sound like much fun for the losers," said Bob.

"No, it certainly wasn't. It was a sacred ritual. They took it very seriously."

Dr. Butterfield led the way on a path under the canopy. A troop of howler monkeys, or baboons as they are called in Belize, was playing on the canopy fifty feet above where branches and vines intertwined linking the trees, up where the bromeliads and orchids grew. Swinging from tree to tree, the baboons were making their distinctive, loud howling sound. A group of tourists were standing below howling back loudly in imitation and provoking the monkeys to make even more noise.

Leaning over towards Bob's ear, Dr. Butterfield whispered, "The large tailless monkeys are usually louder than their smaller cousins. I wonder if they know how ridiculous they look."

It was good he said this, as Bob was just getting ready to let out a little howl himself, which he barely choked back, breaking out in a loud cough.

The path followed by Bob and Dr. Butterfield meandered through ferns and philodendrons that took root on the humus and rotting leaves on the forest floor. As they walked, Bob asked Dr. Butterfield a few questions he had been storing up.

"On the way here on the river, I saw some white men in a boat who were dressed kind of old-fashioned. Who were they?"

"Oh, you saw some of the Old Colony Mennonites from Shipyard. They came here from Canada in the late 1950s. They are the most conservative of all the Mennonites, remaining apart even from their more progressive brethren. They still wear traditional dress and don't use any modern technologies like cars and electricity."

"How can they possibly make their living here in the jungle?"

"They're not like us North Americans. They have a very simple lifestyle. It doesn't take much to sustain them. They can get by on logging and a little farming."

"Well, to each his own. I was also wondering about this jade head I saw a picture of somewhere," said Bob, trying to remember exactly how the blurry green image had been imprinted on his mind.

"You must have been drinking Belikan Beer," laughed Dr. Butterfield. "That's the famous jade statue of the Sun God, Kinich Ahau, that you saw. It was carved around 600 A.D. Standing six inches high and weighing almost 10 pounds, it's the largest jade Mayan artifact ever recovered. My mentor at the Royal Ontario Museum, David Pendergast, was the lucky one who found it buried under the Temple of the Masonry Altars at Altun Ha. That is about twenty-five miles due east of here off the old Northern Highway. If you want to see the jade head, you have to make an appointment to visit the Department of Archeology in Belmopan. The Belize Government keeps the statue there locked up in a vault."

"I can imagine. It must be so valuable. How much do you think it's worth?" asked Bob curiously.

"It's really priceless," replied Dr. Butterfield, wrinkling his brow in thought, "but if forced to put a round number on it, I would say at least ten million dollars."

"Wow!" exclaimed Bob.

Dr. Butterfield scowled. The scholar in him was repelled at the thought that some people were more impressed by the monetary value of the jade head than its significance as an irreplaceable cultural treasure.

Bob couldn't get the jade head out of his mind as they walked the remaining short distance to the Indian Church. He was intrigued by it, and not only by its value. Outside the village, they came upon the crumbling walls of two Spanish missions.

"This is all that's left of the Spanish presence in this area of the world. They came here, starting in 1544, to convert the Mayans to Christianity. But in 1640, the Indians revolted and burned the church down. The Spanish built another church using the stones from one of the temples at Lamanai, but the Indians tore it down too. That stelae over there, which was erected afterwards, contains a rather virulent Mayan denunciation of Christianity. Apparently, the cruelty and greed of the Spanish conquistadors and the friars who accompanied them left the Mayans unconvinced of the truth and virtue of our sacred Christian religion in comparison to their own pagan tomfoolery, if I may be permitted to paraphrase Ambrose Bierce.

"There is also the ruins of a nineteenth-century sugar mill over there complete with rusting metal boilers and storage chambers. It was built in 1866 by former Confederate soldiers from the United States who established sugar plantations nearby. The mill was destroyed a year later by Mayan forces led by General Marcus Canul from Mexico. The Mayan army got as far as Orange Walk Town before it was routed by a troop of Confederate soldiers with modern rifles who shot General Canul right out of his saddle and slaughtered many of the Indians."

"There's certainly a lot of unusual history associated with this site. It's strange to think of Confederate troops down here fighting Maya. My great great grandaddy fought in the Union Army. He might have fought against some of those same soldiers. One of them might've even shot him in the ass at Shiloh," said Bob, referring to the only time a member of his family had ever earned a Purple Heart.

Dr. Butterfield walked Bob back to the boat dock where the rest of the group was already being shepherded into the boat by Fernando. After thanking the learned archeologist profusely, Bob hastened to the end of the dock to claim the last seat in the boat. It would be a long and tiring journey back to Ambergrise Caye. They wouldn't get there until after dusk.

❧

The trip to Lamanai had worn Bob out. He easily fell back into Wally's leisurely routine over the next few days while he rested up. The two of them lounged together on the porch under the palm trees, consuming prodigious quantities of libations and take-out food while generously solving most of the world's problems, at least to their own satisfaction. Gideon stopped by every day or so to see if he could interest Bob in some fishing or snorkeling. But Bob didn't take the bait. He needed the time to think about what he wanted to do next. Maybe he should get in touch with the local Rotarians and check out their project for crippled children before his money ran out, he thought. After all, that's why he told Donna he was coming down here in the first place. He'd better have something to report the next time he talked to her on the telephone or she would think he was just goofing off or maybe worse. When was the last time he'd talked to her? he wondered. A couple of days? A week? He really couldn't remember. Down here time flowed like a lazy river.

"I was thinking, Wally, I might go into Belize City for a while," said Bob, between sips of planter's punch.

"Why would you want to do that?" asked Wally, suddenly sitting bolt upright in his chair and looking startled. "It's just a dirty, smelly, crime-infested town. It's so nice and peaceful out here on our little island. I can't understand why anybody would want to leave. And certainly not to go to Belize City."

"I told the Rotary Club back home that I'd look into a project they have down here to help crippled children."

"That all sounds very nice, but you don't seem like the do-gooder type to me."

"Well, ...I'm not really, but it would give me a chance to meet some people down here and maybe help out a bit. Can you get me a cheap place to stay there for a couple of weeks?"

"Sure, a friend of mine named Elsa has a small guest house in the Fort George area of the city. If I were you, it's the only part of town I'd set my foot in if I valued my life. Yeah, she'll be glad to put you up. But I guarantee you that you'll be back here in a couple of days asking me why I ever let you leave this paradise to go to a hell hole like B-Town as they call it."

"You're probably right, but, what the hell, it's only a twenty-minute flight away, right?" said Bob taking another drink of punch. "It's not like I'm going to China. I can always come back here and take refuge if it's too much for me to take."

10

Ever since she was a girl, Donna had been close to her mother. The relationship had grown even stronger since her father's death a few years ago. But, even so, there were the little inter-generational frictions that cropped up. Donna worried a lot about her mother. Even though the older lady was only in her sixties, she had several chronic ailments including diabetes, arthritis and high blood pressure, which had taken their toll on her already frail body. Her mother's failing health placed quite a burden on Donna as the only child. Like the dutiful daughter she was, she checked in regularly to see if there was anything she could do to help her mother out.

"Hi, Mom," Donna said, as she walked into the kitchen of her mother's new house, which was only a few blocks away.

"Oh, Donna, thanks for coming by," said her mother, hurriedly butting out a cigarette in the sink.

"You're not smoking again, are you?" Donna asked, smelling the smoke. Her mother looked sheepish like an adolescent caught in the act behind the barn.

"Oh, well!" huffed Donna, a bit exasperated. "I can't make you stop. If you want to kill yourself, I guess it's your business. I didn't come here to lecture you, but to see if you needed any groceries."

"There are a few things. The list is on the table."

"Okay, I'll pick them up for you this afternoon."

"Thanks. You look kinda rundown today, Donna. Is anything the matter?"

"I've been having a rough time lately. First Bob leaves. Then I lose my job. Now it's Sarah and her new boyfriend. I don't know what to do."

"I sometimes feel that way too since your father died. A woman needs to have a man around to comfort her."

"Oh, Mom, that's an old fashioned view. It's different nowadays. Woman are more independent. We don't always need to have a man hanging around all the time like women used to think in the old days."

"You don't look very independent to me today."

"I'm coping, Mom."

"Can you get me some cigarettes at the store?"

"Oh, Mom, you are incorrigible. You know how I feel about that."

"Well, no harm in asking."

Donna rolled her eyes and huffed as she went out the door with the list in her hand. It wasn't bad enough to have to deal with Sarah, she thought, but Mom as well. Like many woman of her generation, she was caught between the demands of a troublesome teenager and an aging parent who insisted on acting like a child.

Donna's old Honda Civic ground and ground, but the motor refused to turn over. Damn, thought Donna, what the hell is wrong this time? It always happens when I have to go somewhere important like work at my new job at Gallagher's. If I don't get there on time, I'll probably get fired before I even get started.

A light went on in Donna's head. She went back into the house and fetched the keys to Bob's Mustang from the drawer in the kitchen. Bob won't mind, she told herself as she went through the kitchen door into the garage where the precious red convertible had been safely stored since Bob's departure. Not this once. She'd be very careful. After she opened the garage door, she unlocked the car door and climbed into the driver's seat. Her feet didn't quite reach the pedals so she adjusted the seat. Then she stuck the keys into the ignition and turned. The car started at once with the throaty roar of its big high-performance V-8 engine and tuned sports exhaust system. Donna backed the car carefully out of the garage. After reaching the street, she remembered it was a convertible. Since it was a beautiful, warm evening, she stopped to put the top down before starting towards Gallagher's. Why not? she thought. I might as well enjoy the ride.

The wind blew her hair as she drove out the highway. What was I thinking? she thought. My hair will be a mess when I get to work. I'll look like an old hag.

When she got to Gallagher's, she pulled into the farthest corner of the lot away from all the other cars and put the roof back up. Flipping down the sun visor and taking a comb out of her purse, she made a last ditch effort to rescue her hairdo and make herself presentable before going in to work.

Gallagher's was still the liveliest place in town on a Wednesday night. But it still wasn't very much fun to be working there as a waitress. The country music was extremely loud and after two or three hours gave Donna a splitting headache. The crowd that made the place pulsate with energy turned into a moving obstacle course that Donna had to traverse without dropping her tray.

"Whoops!" said Donna as a man in a Loganville High School jacket with an "85" on the sleeve backed into her causing the tray she was carrying with a sixty-ounce pitcher and four beer mugs to wobble perilously.

"Excuse me, ma'am," he said.

"That's okay. Don't worry about it," said Donna. At least, he's polite, she thought. Some people here act like they're at a slam dance.

Donna worked her way across the room. When she got about halfway, someone yelled from a table at the side, "Hey, waitress! Come on over, we need to order some food."

"I'll be right back," said Donna.

"Well, make it snappy. We can't wait all day. We're starvin' over here," another voice yelled.

Donna finally got over to the table that had ordered the pitcher of beer.

"Put the pitcher down here," said the drunk man dressed in a denim shirt, motioning to an empty place on the table. "Why don't you join us, baby? You can sit here on my lap," he said making three obscene pelvic thrusts.The other three men laughed uproariously. Donna tried to be businesslike and ignored the comment.

"Are you gonna pay now, or do you want to run a tab?" Donna asked.

"We thought you'd do it for free," the man laughed.

"Do I need to bring my manager over here?" Donna asked. "Or are you guys gonna behave?"

"No, no, we'll be good boys and pay," the man said giving her a twenty.

From his response, Donna could tell that he knew the manager was a giant of a man who also served as the bouncer and would like nothing better than to kick a little obnoxious ass.

"You can keep the change," the man said referring to the small change that would be left over after the bill was paid.

"Thank you, sir," said Donna sarcastically, putting the coins in her change belt. The man didn't know just how close Donna had come to pouring the pitcher right over the top of his greasy head.

That night Donna didn't have any other customers that scored quite so high on the slime scale. Several other men tried to hit on her as usual, of course, but at least they were polite and kept their paws to themselves. By closing time at two o'clock, Donna just had to get out of there. Her head throbbed. Her feet were sore from all the running around in high heels. And all her muscles ached from carrying so many heavy trays. Another night in the life of a working mom, she thought. It was only the one hundred fifty dollars she got in tips that made the job bearable.

Donna's ordeals for the night were not over yet. To her horror, when she went out to the parking lot, she found the whole side of Bob's precious Mustang all smashed in. A dent highlighted by an unsightly strip of white paint ran the full length of the car. Somebody with a few too many must have sideswiped it on their way out of the parking lot. Oh, no! she thought. Bob's going to be really mad. There was no way she could afford to get it fixed before he got back. The insurance was in his name and he would have to make the claim, that is, if he'd kept the insurance up. About this, she was doubtful, given the shaky financial position Bob was in when he left and the fact that he wasn't planning on using the car.

Sarah's boyfriend Joe lived in a two-story brick house on the other side of the tracks that belonged to the "Hell's Riders" motorcycle club. The house was surrounded by a chain link fence and had security cameras mounted on the corners of the building. It was late on a Thursday night and the club members were sitting around drinking beer and watching television on a torn vinyl couch in a room littered with empty beer cans and discarded take-out food containers. The phone rang. A man with tattoos all over his big, ugly, oversized arms and a tank top that barely covered his fat belly answered.

"Okay, okay, Fuckin' A," he said abruptly and hung up.

Turning to Joe, he said, "The boss wants us to deliver a package over to Champaign to sell to the college pricks. I want you to take it over tonight."

"Why me?" asked Joe. "I'm too tired. Why don't you get Sonny to do it?"

"Lissen, fuckhead, I'm not asking you. I'm tellin' you," said Jocko.

"Okay, okay, shit, I'll do it. Gimme the package."

Jocko went into the back room and came out with a package he handed to Joe.

"This is a big job for our club. Don't fuck it up."

"Yeah, don't worry," said Joe.

Joe went out the back door with the package and put it in the saddlebag of his Harley. Then he was off with a roar and a squeal. On his way out of town he was passing through the black neighborhood and he saw a 7-Eleven still open. Better get some cigarettes, he thought. It will be a fuckin' long ride.

Joe walked into the store and went up to the counter. A large black man with slightly oriental features who looked about thirty was standing behind the counter.

"What can I get for you?" he said in heavily-accented, sing-songy English.

"Two packs of Camels," said Joe.

"Okay," said the black man, picking two packs of cigarettes off the display behind the counter and giving them to Joe. "That will be eight dollars and fifty cents, please."

Joe searched in his jeans pockets, but came up empty. Shit, he thought, I left my wallet back at the house. "'Fraid I don't have any money," he said.

"Then you can give me back the cigarettes."

"No, I'll pay you later."

"No, you give me back the cigarettes now. We don't give credit."

"Lissen, nigger," said Joe, starting to get mad. "You see the emblem on this jacket. You don't want to mess with us."

"I don't care what stupid picture you have on your jacket. Give me back the cigarettes," said the black man, grabbing Joe's hand and simultaneously pushing the alarm under the counter.

Joe reached into his pocket and pulled out a gun with his free hand. The black man grabbed that hand too, forcing Joe to drop the gun. Pulling on Joe's arms, he dragged him over the counter and onto the floor. When the black man let him go, Joe tried to get up to hit him. Big mistake! The last thing Joe felt was a giant black fist smashing into his face like a sledgehammer. Pow! When he woke up, and the stars before his eyes cleared, he found himself looking into the face of a white policeman standing over him with a gun. Another burly black policeman was speaking to the black man.

"Thanks, Van," he said. "We've been trying to get something on the 'Hell's Riders' for some time. The package in his saddlebags is a real catch for us. Facing hard time, our friend on the floor might be willing to inform on some of the other gang members. Who knows? If we're lucky, we may even be able to trace it all the way back to the supplier. The DEA tells us he transships cocaine through Belize from Columbia."

"That's good," said Van. "Since I've come here from Vietnam, I've seen too many drugs for sale. I don't like these bad guys. They sell drugs to children like that kid who died just a few weeks ago. Someone has to stop them."

11

Manuel took Bob to the airport for the eight o'clock flight off the island. Wally had been still sleeping when Bob left. That was good as Wally preferred hellos to good-byes. The twenty-minute flight to the Belize City Municipal Airport was routine until it came time to land. A man ran out on the runway and started waving his hands wildly. The small plane had to pull up sharply and circle while two uniformed men chased the man off the runway.

"What's going on?" Bob asked the pilot sitting just in front of him.

"Oh! No problem, maan," he said. "It's just crazy ole Al. He likes to run out on the runway when nobody's looking and try to flag down the planes. He must've seen a war movie about an aircraft carrier or something. It won't take the boys long to run him off."

On the second pass, the runway was clear as predicted. The plane was able to land, but had to buck a strong side wind coming off the water. Waves lapped over the breakwaters at the side of the runway. But what else would you expect from an airstrip built at sea-level right next to the water?

Bob climbed down out of the plane and stood on the tarmac waiting while a man unloaded the baggage compartment. His bag was one of the first out. Picking it up, he walked out through the small wooden terminal building that looked something like a large converted garage with the paint peeling off. One of the waiting cab drivers took his bag and motioned him into an old green Buick with the chrome strip missing on the side and duct tape holding on the mirror.

"Where you be goin', maan?" asked the big Creole driver in a white shirt and grey slacks.

"Elsa's Guest House," replied Bob.

"If you say so, boss, but if I were you I'd be goin' to the Princess or the Fort George."

The cab sped quickly down Barrack Road along the Sea Wall to the Old Fort George area of the city. The houses were mostly built in Caribbean style of whitewashed wood with verandahs, shuttered windows and orange tin roofs. In the heavily-treed heart of the Fort George area, the houses got larger and more imposing with big steps going up to the main floor verandahs. The driver pulled up in front of one of these impressive, but slightly shabby, colonial structures bearing a small discreet sign announcing "Elsa's Guest House." A bougainvillea covered in purple flowers bloomed in the small front yard behind the white fence. After paying the driver, Bob got out and, bag in hand, walked through the gate and up the long steps. Standing on the porch, he knocked lightly on the door. Soon an immense black lady in a yellow and orange, flower-print dress, which made her look even bigger and more imposing, came to the door.

"Come on in," she said, flashing a big smile. "I'd been 'spectin' you. I'm Elsa."

"Pleased to meet you, Elsa," said Bob.

"Wally said I should give you our best room and our lowest price," said Elsa. "Any friend of Wally is a friend of mine. Follow me, we can take care of business later."

"Did you ever meet Wally?' Bob asked curiously.

"No, I haven't. He's never come to town. I only talk to him on the phone."

"Of course," said Bob. "I should have guessed."

Bob followed Elsa up a second long staircase to the second story. She led him down a hallway to a big room in the front with a large window looking out onto Memorial Park and to the sea beyond. The room had a large bed with a headboard, a writing desk and chair, and a couch and coffee table with a vase of freshly cut purple flowers from the front yard on top.

"The bathroom's down the hall and breakfast is in the main dining room downstairs between seven and nine o'clock," she announced as she waddled backwards out of the room.

"Thank you," replied Bob, laying his bag on the floor in the corner next to the closet. Plenty of time, he thought, to freshen up and to get over to the Fort George for the usual Wednesday, Rotary Club lunch that Wally had told him about. That would be the easiest way to hook up with the local Rotary and to meet some people. If he was going to do anything for the crippled children's project, he'd better get started soon before he ran out of money.

❧

A few hours later, Bob, dressed in the one wrinkled blue seersucker suit that had been laying unused in the bottom of his bag since he had arrived in Belize, strolled across the park to the Fort George Hotel, feeling quite jaunty for a change. He walked up the ramp past a few Belizean men sitting on the curb with assortments of carved wooden boats and wildlife.

"Hey, maan, wanna buy a souvenir?" asked the young one holding a dolphin carved out of the hard dark zirocote wood favored by local carvers.

"No, thanks," said Bob, going through the doors into the lobby, which was paneled in dark wood and decorated with enormous wooden sculptures.

At the desk, Bob asked the clerk where the Rotary meeting was to be held and was sent up the stairs to the main dining room. It was at the end of the hall and had large windows looking out over the pool and garden onto the water. When he entered the room, he was greeted by a short, distinguished-looking black man in a blue suit."Welcome to our weekly meeting. I'm Coleman Butler, the local chapter president," he said in a very British accent that singled him out as a member of the Creole elite created by the intermarriage of the English Baymen and free Africans.

"Pleased to meet you. I'm Bob Wayne. I'm a guest from the Loganville, Illinois, chapter."

"Oh, yes," said Mr. Butler. "I'd heard you would be coming. We've had a lot of guests here from Illinois because of the crippled children project."

"I hope we haven't been abusing your hospitality," said Bob.

"Oh, no," said Mr. Butler. "We're pleased to make so many new friends. And it's essential for the success of the project."

"By the way, who's the local contact for the project?" asked Bob.

"Neville Jones. The man himself is standing right over there. Do you want me to introduce you?"

"Sure. I'd love to meet him."

Mr. Butler escorted Bob over to Mr. Jones and introduced them, before excusing himself to take up his official greeting post back at the door.

"I'm glad to meet you," said Bob. "I'd like to talk to you about the crippled children project. When I told Dr. Sherman I was coming down here and that I was an accountant, he said there might be something I could do to help you out with the books."

"You bet there is," said Mr. Jones. "I'm afraid they're in pretty rough shape. We've been waiting for you anxiously ever since Mr. Sherman wrote to tell us that you would be coming to help us."

"Well, I hope I'll be able to help you out and you won't be disappointed."

"Why don't we sit down. We can talk more over lunch."

Mr. Jones led Bob over to the head table near the window. A blue orchid sat in a small vase in the middle of the table to distinguish it from the others. There they took their seats with Mr. Butler and another tall, lean, athletic-looking black gentleman.

"I'm glad you could join us, Mr. Wayne. Permit me to introduce you to Mr. Nigel McKie. We're fortunate to have him as our speaker today. He is going to tell us about the basketball game he is organizing for next summer. One of our fine local Belizean teams is going to play a pickup team made up of a few former NBA players and some U.S. college stars. The game's always popular down here and fills up the Civic Auditorium. Everyone gets a real kick out of watching the U.S. All Stars blow their tops when they discover the Belizeans are no pushovers. After that, the game gets really interesting. The profits from the game go to support local amateur athletics. Mr. McKie himself used to play basketball, you know. Are you going to join the boys this year, Nigel?"

"No, I'm afraid I'm getting a bit old for that, Coleman, bad knees and all, you know. But I always like coming back home to Belize just the same."

"Mr. Wayne is joining us here from the state that's the home of the Chicago Bulls and Michael Jordan, the greatest basketball player to ever lace up a pair of Nikes."

"Pleased to meet you," said Mr. McKie. "Do you like basketball?"

"Sure...to watch," said Bob. "Even in my prime I wasn't much of a player. I spent most of my high school career on the bench and I haven't played in years."

"Don't worry," laughed Mr. McKie. "I'm not trying to recruit you to the All Star team. We already have enough American players without you. And they are all a lot taller."

"Well, I wasn't exactly a dwarf in high school, but I know what you mean. Six feet tall certainly wouldn't cut it in the NBA these days," replied Bob.The Rotary Club meeting at the Fort George was very much the same as the one in Loganville—the prayer, the songs, the chicken, the announcements, and the speaker. If it weren't for the Belize flag, which was blue with red stripes on the top and bottom and the national crest in the middle, and for the rice and beans served with the chicken, it could have been somewhere in the United States. The Rotary Club is a marvelous thing, thought Bob. It's the same everywhere—kind of like a McDonald's for business and professional people.

During their lunch, Bob learned about all of the Rotary Club's activities in Belize, including the crippled children project. Neville Jones invited Bob to come over to his office later in the week to talk about the books and to make arrangements to do some work.

An added benefit for Bob was that Mr. McKie turned out to be a very entertaining speaker. He regaled the small audience of about thirty men and women with the story of how he, as a poor boy from Belize City, was able to get a basketball scholarship to study at a U.S. Division 1 college in Massachusetts and to make it into the NBA. True, he mostly sat on his ass on the bench for his three-year career, but he had made a pile of money and launched himself into a lucrative career in public relations. Now he was using his good fortune and organizational talents to benefit other young Belizeans athletes.

Bob went back to the guest house happy to have met a few more nice people. He now had a place he could go to on Wednesdays while he was here in Belize City where he would feel right at home.

⁂

That night Bob was sitting on the couch back in his room at Elsa's thumbing through the guidebook on Belize he'd bought at the airport. Putting down the book, he began to think of Donna and how much he missed her. For the first time since he was in Belize, he felt alone. Maybe I should call Donna, he thought. I finally have something concrete to report, other than drinking and relaxing that is. Picking up the phone, he dialed the familiar number.

"Hello," Donna answered at the other end.

"Hi, Donna, it's me."

"Oh, hi, Bob, where are you calling from?"

"I'm in Belize City now, staying at a place called Elsa's Guest House. It's not bad. You'd like it. It's kind of like a bed and breakfast."

"Have you met the people from the Rotary Club yet?"

Bob knew she was going to ask that. Woman are so suspicious. He was wise to have waited to call her."Yeah, funny you'd ask. In fact, I just met them today. They're very nice people. Later this week I'm gonna go over to see one of them and talk about the work they want me to do."

"That's good. Willya be able to come home soon?"

"I don't know. It may take a while yet. I'm sure you can get along for a little longer without me around."

"I miss you very much, though, and wish you'd come home."

"I miss you, too, honey."

"I have some good new and bad news," Donna reported.

"Start with the bad."

"The bad news is I lost my job at Ellie's. The good news is I got another working as a waitress at Gallagher's."

"That's all good news," said Bob. "You never liked Ellie much anyway."

"Yeah, but the new job is really hard work. I have to be on my feet for so many hours. And some of the customers are so rude and demanding."

"Oh, you'll get used to it."

"Come home soon."

"I'll try. By the way, are you taking good care of my Mustang?"

"Sorry. Gotta go, Bob, can't talk any more. Sarah's calling me. Anyway, this call must be costing you a lot of money."

"Yeah, it is. Okay, good-bye, Donna."

It was good to hear Donna's voice. He'd forgotten how sweet she sounded. Bob wished they could have talked longer. Strange though how anxious she was to get off the phone, he thought.

12

Later that night, around ten o'clock, Bob wandered over to the Baymen's Tavern in the Fort George Hotel for a nightcap. After several weeks with Wally, he had developed a strong craving for hard refreshment before turning in. The bar was on the second floor of the hotel looking out over the water. But at night not much could be seen except for the sodium lights on the hotel's dock and the sparkling string of light bulbs on the boom of a large yacht anchored further out in the deeper water.

Bob went into the bar and took a seat at a small table near the window. Soon a young waiter in a green tropical shirt came over to his table to take his order. Bob asked for a daiquiri just like Hemingway used to drink at El Floridita. While he was waiting for his drink to arrive, he looked around the room and took stock of the other customers. There were two well-dressed Latino-looking men engaged in a heated discussion in one corner of the room, two Creole Belizean Defense Force officers with flirty young Creole women in tight dresses, an attractive Spanish-looking woman drinking by herself at a table close to the bar, and a single middle-aged man in a white linen suit at the table right next to his. Bob couldn't help making eye contact with the man.

"You're new around here?" the man inquired in a southern drawl.

"Yeah," said Bob. "I'm just down here for a few weeks to look around. What about you?"

"I live here. Part of the year, anyway."

"Where about?" said Bob as the waiter deposited his drink on the table.

"I have a place up toward Orange Walk Town. Where are you staying?"

"At a small guest house near here."

"You care to join me for a drink?"

"Sure, it would be a pleasure," said Bob, picking up his drink and moving over to the man's table. "I'm Bob Wayne. With whom do I have the honor of sharing a drink?"

"I'm Nick Devlin," the man said, tipping his drink in Bob's direction.

Well, one drink turned into another and still more. The next thing Bob knew it was midnight and he was outside the hotel with Nick climbing into the back seat of a black Jeep Grand Cherokee with dark tinted windows. The driver was a husky-looking young Garifuna man in a light blue tropical-weight suit and open-neck shirt named Jules. Garifunas, known as Black Caribs, are the descendants of escaped African slaves and Caribbean Indians who had been driven out of St. Vincent by the British and had taken refuge in the Belizean town of Dangriga, just down the coast from Belize City at the mouth of Stann Creek. Bob noticed that the driver was wearing a wooden talisman on a leather necklace around his neck. But what he didn't know was that it had been prepared by a buyei or shaman in an ancient Obeah ritual brought over from Africa. Its purpose was to provide protection against evil spirits and the other more physical threats Jules might encounter in carrying out his duties as Nick's bodyguard.

Nick had convinced Bob to accompany him to the Princess Hotel and Casino where they both were going to try their luck at a few games of chance. This wasn't very hard as Bob had been to Vegas a few times and had trouble passing up the opportunity to gamble in a real casino.

The casino at the Princess Hotel was crowded and smoky. Most of the casually-dressed clientele came from the cruise ship anchored out beyond the reef. They had been ferried in by a fleet of tenders to the hotel's marina. There were only a few locals in the casino and they were much better dressed than the tourists in their drip-dry clothes. The room was filled with slot machines, and crap, roulette and card tables—the usual stock-in-trade of any casino. Lights flashed, machines pinged and ponged, change jingled in buckets. People were clustered around the various gambling stations. Some gamblers were quiet and morose, engrossed in their own private world, compulsively pumping coins into slot machines or silently playing cards. Others were more noisy, gathered around the craps or roulette tables. They were mostly watching the few adventuresome enough to risk their money by daring to pick up the dice or put their chips on a number, egging them on and roaring appreciatively when someone won big.

"Good evening, Mr. Devlin, it is good to see you again. If there's anything you need, just let me know," said a tuxedo-clad gentleman with a foreign accent.

"Thanks, Hassan," said Nick. "You can be sure I will."

"What's your game?" Nick asked Bob.

"Let's start out with a little cards," said Bob.

"Okay," said Nick. "Give me a couple hundred and I'll send my man Jules here over to the wicket to get us some chips."

Reaching into his back pocket, Bob pulled out his wallet and took out ten twenty dollar bills, which represented most of his remaining cash. He held the money in his hand for a minute, looking at it wistfully before surrendering it to Nick. "This is about twice my usual limit and I'm running a little short of cash," he said. "I'm not a high-roller, you know."

Nick grabbed the money out of Bob's hand. Reaching into his own pocket with his other hand, he pulled out a roll of twenties, and shuffled them in with Bob's as if he was dealing with a deck of cards rather than money."Don't worry. This is gonna be your lucky night," said Nick, handing Jules the neat stack of twenty dollar bills.

"Let's go over to the blackjack tables and get warmed up," said Nick.

"Why not?" said Bob, trying to suppress the butterflies in his stomach.

They soon found a table with two empty seats. The dealer was an attractive young Creole woman wearing a low top that displayed her ample cleavage. There were four decks in the sleeve in front of her, all shuffled and ready to go. This was standard practice in most casinos as it made it much more difficult for card counters to keep track when four decks were in play. But for amateurs like Bob this precaution wasn't really necessary. The dealer herself was enough of a distraction to foil any attempts he might make at card counting even if he had known how to do it.

By the time Bob and Nick got comfortable in their seats, Jules was back with a stack of five-dollar chips for each of them. Bob got the smaller stack. They anted up and the night of gambling was officially underway. Jules stood discreetly behind them and kept watch, a cigarette dangling jauntily from his mouth. After about an hour, they had consumed several complimentary drinks and had both parlayed their initial stakes into a tidy profit. The time had come to raise the bet. Bob anted up four chips. He was dealt two aces and doubled down, splitting his hand in two and putting down four more chips. The dealer dealt him a Jack of spades on one and a Queen of hearts on the other. Incredible luck—double blackjack!

"You must be bringing me some real luck," Bob said to Nick, as he raked in the chips.

"Stick with me, man, and it's only the beginning. Now let's go play some real cards."

In the back of the room there was a table for high-stakes draw poker beckoning. Only two of the four seats were occupied—one by an elderly American from the cruise ship wearing a blue blazer and cravat, another by a middle-aged Creole man with a gold chain in the neck of his purple silk shirt. At the table, the minimum bet was twenty dollars. Nick escorted Bob over to an empty seat to the right of the dealer and bade him to sit down. Taking the other empty seat to the left of the dealer, he looked ready for action. Again Jules watched protectively over his boss, while he puffed away.

The dealer was a Turkish man with a mustache and large, well-manicured hands. From the way he handled the cards, you could tell he was a real professional. Bob arranged his chips neatly in the holders in front of him and began to play. Winning some hands and losing some, the card game continued indecisively for a half hour. Bob was getting tired and the free drinks were starting to catch up with him, but he continued to play and anted up again anyway. After the cards were dealt face down, he picked up his hand. Three jacks—diamonds, hearts and clubs—a ten of hearts, and an eight of spades. Why not go for it? he thought, boldly laying two hundred dollars on the table. The two other men matched him. Nick saw his two hundred and raised another one hundred. The other two men and the house threw in the extra one hundred dollars. Bob discarded the eight and drew a jack of spades. Trying hard not to reveal his good luck, he constrained himself and only bet one hundred dollars. The old man looked disappointed and folded, but the Creole and Nick and the house were still in. Bob laid his cards on the table, four jacks. The Creole only had a pair of eights and a pair of aces. He had tried for a full house and come up short, but had stubbornly stuck it out anyway. Nick had a full house, kings and sevens. The dealer laid his hand on the table—four nines. The pot was Bob's.

"Let's cash out our chips while I still have some and get the hell out of here. Your luck is better than mine tonight," said Nick.

"It sure is. Now is a good time to quit before it runs out," said Bob.

When Bob walked away from the wicket, he had almost two thousand dollars in his pocket. Things were starting to look up. He could now afford to stay a few more weeks without going deeper into the hole. This would give him the time he needed to do the job he promised for the crippled children's project. He'd have some explaining to do if he had to go home before he finished the job he had come down for.

"Why don't you come out and see my boat?" said Nick as they walked out of the casino. "We can have a drink there and then I'll get Jules to drop you off at the Fort George dock afterwards. I have a launch docked here at the marina that can take us out."

"Okay," said Bob. "After winning all this money, I'm so pumped up I couldn't sleep anyway."

Jules had the launch already untied with the powerful Mercury inboard motor idling when they got out on the dock in the marina behind the hotel. It was a short ride out to the anchored yacht across the calm moonlit water inside the reef.

Nick's yacht was much more than Bob had expected. It was huge and luxurious.

"Wow!" said Bob as he climbed up the ladder onto the deck. "What is this, anyway?"

"It's an old reconditioned sixty-six foot Burger Flybridge Cruiser. It has three staterooms, a galley and dinette, and a large aft deck with a wet bar. There's also a two-berth stateroom for the crew. That's where Jules is going now. I find it to be a quite comfortable place to stay when I'm in Belize City. I've even done a bit of cruising around the Caribbean and back home to New Orleans. Its twin 464 horsepower diesel engines aren't powerful enough to make it a speedboat, but they enable it to cruise at almost fourteen knots."

Bob followed Nick along the railing and through the small door into the aft deck. Nick took his jacket off and threw it over one of the chairs.

"I'm getting a little bit sick of all those fruity rum concoctions they drink around here. How does a nice single malt scotch sound to you? I've got a fifth of Glennfidich sitting right over there."

"I've had so much booze tonight that you may be wasting it on me, but go ahead," said Bob, collapsing into one of the deck chairs.

Nick poured them both a scotch on the rocks and brought the two drinks over and put them on the glass-topped table next to Bob's chair. Bob noticed a small shamrock with the letters AB inside tattooed on the back of his right forearm. Must be Irish or something, he thought. Nick walked around and sat down in the chair on the other side of the table. Bob picked up the tumbler and took a swig. It was smooth, but fiery. He enjoyed the way it burned as it slid down his throat.

"What exactly do you do that you can afford to live like this?" asked Bob, letting his curiosity get the better of his discretion.

"I have some businesses here—a sugar plantation, a few citrus groves, an interest in a couple of small hotels. You know, a little of this and a little of that. Put it all together, I do all right. What about you? I'd heard you are an accountant. Is that true?"

"Yeah, but who told you?"

"Oh, somebody at the Fort George Hotel. They know everybody's business here even if you're just passing through. I tell you the walls have ears in that hotel."

"I'm not even staying there," protested Bob.

"Oh, don't worry about it. You know I could use the services of a good accountant to help me computerize the books of my various businesses. I'm afraid it has become a bit of a mess and sometimes even I don't know how I'm doing. I didn't want to get anybody down here to help me though, because they all have such fucking big mouths. You're just passing through though and I suppose you can keep things to yourself if I make it worth your while."

"Sounds interesting," said Bob. "I'd like to stay down here awhile longer and making some money would definitely help. It would be nice to try out a real first class hotel like the Fort George before I go home. But before I can do any work for you, I have a little job I have to do for the Rotary Club."

"I hope they're paying you well," said Nick.

"Not really, it's pro bono," said Bob.

"Pro bono, what the hell does that mean?"

"It means I'm doing it to help a worthy cause."

"Okay, if you want to waste your time, I can't stop you. How long will it take?"

"Not long."

"That's good. We can talk more about my job later when you're done. For now, let's get back to celebrating tonight's winnings at the gaming tables. Have you ever tried any of this?" said Nick reaching into a drawer in the table and pulling out a small plastic bag containing white powder.

"Is that what I think it is?" asked a surprised Bob.

"Yup, you ever tried it?" he asked, pouring some out on the small mirror on top of the table.

"No, I've only smoked the odd joint in college."

"Then now is a good time to try some," Nick said, dividing the pile of powder up into neat rows with a razor that he took from the plastic sack.

Nick picked up the mirror and snorted one of the lines up his nose using a rolled-up hundred dollar bill. He coughed a bit and then handed the mirror and another hundred dollar bill to Bob.

"Your turn," he said.

"Why the hundred dollar bill?' asked Bob.

"Oh, it's customary back home in the United States," said Nick. "And we don't want to break with tradition just cause we're down here in the boonies, do we?"

"I guess not, if you put it that way," replied Bob.

Looking a little hesitant, but not wanting to lose face in front of his new-found friend, Bob took the mirror, put the hundred up his nose, and inhaled a line. At first he didn't feel anything, but gradually a feeling of euphoria came over him. The night passed quickly as the two of them took turns snorting lines. Morning found them still sitting on the deck together, but much the worse for the wear. While they both looked like they were about to collapse, they couldn't sleep. That's what cocaine does to you. It will rev you up and burn you out if you let it.

Nick said, "We gotta stop. I've got some business to do today. I'm gonna wake Jules up to take me into the Fort George after I freshen up a bit. You can go into one of the staterooms and try to get some sleep if you'd like."

"Okay," said Bob weakly. "I've had it." After a while, he staggered off to the stateroom and crashed on the bed.

While Bob couldn't really sleep well with the cocaine and alcohol in his system, he laid around in a stupor until sometime in the mid-afternoon. Then, starting to take more of an interest in his surroundings, he began to looked around the cabin. The only light in the room came through a single small porthole. He got up out of the bunk and went over to look out. Peering through the small round window, he could see the Fort George across the water. How did I get out here? he asked himself. Then his memory gradually started to come back. He remembered Nick and the casino and coming out on the boat. But his head was still foggy and he couldn't remember the details. What he needed was some air. He went out the door and down the hall towards the aft deck. There he was greeted by a mellifluous voice.

"Hiya, sugar," it said.

Bob's eyes were not yet accustomed to the bright sun so he squinted to see who the voice was coming from. There tanning on one of the deck chairs was a stunning Creole beauty in a white bikini that contrasted perfectly with her milk-chocolate skin. She smelled sweetly of coconut from the suntan oil that made her body so appealingly smooth and shiny.

"Oh, hello," said Bob, a bit taken aback by what seemed like an apparition.

"Nick told me to expect to see you before the afternoon was over," she said. "My name's Luna. Luna Williams."

"Mine's Bob Wayne," he said, looking at her delicately featured face with almost oriental-looking eyes.

"Yeah, I know," she said. "Why don't you pull up a chair and sit down?"

"Okay," said Bob, dropping in the chair next to her. "What are you doing out here?"

"Me?" she said, smiling warmly. "Why I'm just enjoying the warm sun and the cool breeze off the water. Nick and I are, shall we say...um...'friends.' "

"I guess I'm his 'friend' too, then."

"Then I'm gonna give you a little friendly warning as one friend to another because you seem like a nice guy. Nick doesn't just have friends like ordinary people. He has a reason for every one of his 'friends.' He's a user, not a giver. I think I know what he wants from me. What does he want from you?"

"I don't know."

"You'll have to wait and see," she said, twisting her braided hair, which was the fashion in the Caribbean.

Although Bob was curious about Luna's warning, he let it pass. His head hurt too much from the excesses of the previous night to pursue it. And now the steady rocking motion of the boat was starting to get to him. All he wanted to do was to get back to dry land before he got sick and embarrassed himself in front of Luna.

"I'd like to stay and talk to you more, but I'm really not feeling very well and need to get back to my hotel," Bob said sheepishly.

"Don't worry. I'll signal for the launch to come out and take you back to the Fort George dock if you want."

"Thanks," said Bob weakly. "I'd be very grateful if you could do that."

It wasn't long before the launch pulled alongside and Bob managed to step in and take a seat. The ride back proved too much for Bob. He puked his guts up over the side all the way back. In the clear water, he could see the swarms of tropical fish attracted by his vomit. As awful as he felt, he consoled himself that at least Luna had not witnessed his indignity.

13

Neville Jones's law office was in one of the old houses right across Cork St. from the Fort George Hotel. When Bob arrived in the morning, a pretty Creole secretary in a tight-fitting tan linen suit announced his arrival and ushered him into an office where he found Neville sitting behind a big mahogany desk in a green leather chair. At the end of the room, there was a similarly upholstered couch and chair with a mahogany coffee table arranged in front. The sienna walls were decorated with prints of Mayan ruins that had been drawn by Frederick Catherwood during his 1839 trip to Central America with John Lloyd Stephens. A golden-colored Persian rug was on the floor.

Neville got out of his chair and greeted Bob heartily. "Good to see you again, Bob. Why don't you come over and sit down on the couch so we can talk?"

No sooner had they sat down then Neville's secretary efficiently reappeared carrying a tray of coffee and laid it on the table for the two men, leaving as quickly as she had come.

"Thank you, Lizzie," said Neville.

The two men put sugar and milk in their coffee to suit their taste and began to drink.

Neville began, "When I say the books for the crippled children are really in a mess, I mean a mess with a capital 'M.' In more than ten years, we've never had anyone prepare proper financial statements. The person who keeps the records for us is a man named Alejandro. All he has is a high school education. He never even took any bookkeeping, let alone accounting courses. But nevertheless he is at least meticulous about keeping all the receipts. He also has done a pretty good job of keeping track of the cash inflows and outflows from the bank account. The problem is that he doesn't know how to prepare an income statement or balance sheet, which, of course, we'll need when we get audited, as we will inevitably be if we are to retain our tax status as a charity. Do you think you can prepare the required financial statements for us?"

"Sure, it's a piece of cake for a real accountant," answered Bob, with a mixture of pride and contempt.

"How long do you think it will take?"

"No more than a week."

"It would be excellent to get it done so quickly. Could you start next week? I can take you up to Belmopan on Monday and pick you up at the end of the week. While we're out there we can go visit Pedro Uck if you like. He's one of the people we've helped and now he's very active in helping us to promote the program. You might've seen the video he's in."

"As a matter of fact, I did when Dr. Sherman spoke at our Rotary Club in Loganville."

"I'll also arrange to have Pedro take us to see Xunantunich. It's a famous Mayan site nearby. I think you'll enjoy seeing it."

"Great, it sounds like fun. I'll look forward to it."

"I would like to take you to see the clinic in Cayo too, but unfortunately it's only active when the doctors come down from the States."

"That's okay. I'm not very interested in medical things anyway."

The next few days passed uneventfully as Bob waited to go to Belmopan. He spent his time looking around the city. At first, he only strolled the tree-shaded streets of the Fort George district admiring the old wooden colonial homes, the Memorial Park, the Fort George Lighthouse. Wally's warning about crime scared him away from venturing downtown. Every time he even got near the Swing Bridge that separates the Fort George District from downtown, a young Rasta Man in a red, yellow and green knit tam, selling marijauna, would hassle him.

"Oy, maan. Praise Jah. Rasta. Dread," said the man.

On the third time this happened, while trying to avoid making eye contact, Bob made the mistake of nodding at the man in recognition.

"You wan bush, maan. I-and-I sell cheap," the man asked, taking advantage of the opening.

"No, thank you."

"Yu giv mi piece of money den," said the man coming closer.

"No."

"Why not? Maan. You rich, I-and-I poor." said the man, looking bigger and more threatening.

"I said no, and I really meant it," asserted Bob, turning and walking back toward the hotel as fast as he could, shaken by his encounter.

The next day, Bob decided that the time had finally come to put aside his fear of the Rasta Man once and for all and cross the bridge. After all, he told himself, I can handle myself pretty well. Didn't I punch Carl in the nose in fourth grade when he called me a wimp? After that the other kids gave me a wide berth. The Rasta Man doesn't know who he is dealing with here. The terror of the Lincoln School playground. I'll just tell him to fuck off, and be done with him.The motivation behind his strengthened desire to go downtown was an article he had seen that morning in *Amandala,* the local weekly newspaper. It told about a special exhibit of Mayan artifacts from the Department of Archeology in Belmopan that was being held at the Bliss Institute. He was curious to see with his own eyes the main attraction of the exhibit, the famous jade statue of the Sun God, Kinich Ahau, in all of its shiny green splendor.

This morning when Bob got to the Swing Bridge, the Rasta Man wasn't there. Breathing a sigh of relief that his new-found pugnacity wasn't going to be tested, Bob ventured onto the bridge. Once on the other side, he went past the new market building that looked like a concrete bunker and into Central Park. Following the diagonal path across the square, he pushed his way through people milling about, food and drink vendors with carts, and taxi drivers standing around waiting for a fare.

The Supreme Court Building stood on the other side of the park. Built as a symbol of British colonial authority in what at the time was one of the Empire's most remote outposts, it still linked the country to its past. A solid two-story white edifice with green trim, it had a clock tower in the middle with the country's coat of arms embossed at the base in the same place where the British crest used to be. Its upper balcony and stairs had a decorative wrought-iron railing, and its lower level, which had to be reached by the imposing staircase, was porticoed. Two black-robed lawyers stood on the landing smoking cigarettes and conferring animatedly.

I wonder what they're talking about, Bob thought. Perhaps, the fate of some poor devil who has had the misfortune to run afoul of the majesty of law. Or maybe only where to have lunch.

While Bob would have liked to indulge his curiosity and go and look inside, he hesitated, intimidated by the building's imposing formality. Instead he continued his walk down towards the water where the Bliss Institute stood. It was built using the money that came out of a trust fund established by an eccentric Englishman. The story is a strange one, which could only have happened in Belize.

The year was 1926. Henry Edward Ernest Victor Bliss, whose title of the Fourth Baron Bliss came from the former Kingdom of Portugal, arrived off the coast of Belize in his yacht *Sea King*. His frail body, which had been stricken with polio as a youth, was already ravaged by food poisoning he had picked up in Trinidad. Too ill to come ashore, the Baron languished on his yacht for several months, passing the time fishing in the harbor while his body grew ever weaker. Belizeans, being nothing if not curious, particularly about things from their erstwhile colonial master England, and not caring that the Baron's title was not a real British hereditary peerage, came out in droves to visit the mystery man on his boat. Their kindness and friendliness so touched the ailing Baron that he left most of his money in trust for good works in Belize. As a consequence, a national holiday was established in his honor, which is celebrated each March 9th with a regatta. Boats of all sizes and shapes, from sleek modern sailing yachts to working fishing dories, assemble off Fort George where the Baron's grave and memorial are located. On land, the custom is for children of all ages to fly multicolored kites. This makes for the kind of colorful spectacle Belizeans love.

Inside the Bliss Institute, Bob slipped quietly past a security guard, who was dozing in a chair, into the special exhibit hall where he admired the pottery and small jade objects found in a glass case. One of the pottery figures looked like a crocodile with a head in its mouth. There were also jade beads for necklaces. In the corner sat a large rectangular high-tech display case containing the glowing-green, softball-sized jade head. Bob walked over and examined it carefully. It was indeed a work of beauty. Who was the Mayan Michelangelo who made it? he wondered. Why did he make it? How had it remained in such perfect shape after being buried for hundreds of years? How many Mayan kings had possessed it before it was buried? What role did it play in the rise and fall of Mayan civilizations? Will its future be as eventful as its past? With these unanswered questions still buzzing around in his head like bees, he left the Institute and wended his way back to the guest house.

When Bob got back to the Swing Bridge, it was half past five. The bridge was being cranked open to let the Haulover-Creek fleet back in from fishing, just as it had every day since 1923 when the bridge had been completed. For the few minutes it took the men to rotate the capstan using long poles, Bob was content to lean over the railing and watch a parade of pastel covered sailboats chug by under the power of their small outboard motors. Once they had passed and the bridge was reopened, he was able to cross.

The Rasta Man was waiting for him on the other side. “Oy, maan,” he said as he walked towards Bob.

“Fu...er...sorry, I’m in a hurry. Can’t talk now,” Bob replied as he hurried away in the direction of Elsa’s. Maybe next time I’ll tell him, Bob thought.

14

The next Monday as planned, Neville Jones pulled up in front of Elsa's in a new brown Toyota SUV. Bob saw him out the window of his upstairs room and rushed down to meet him. They were going out to Belmopan for a few days to the office that housed the books for the Rotary Club's Belize project for crippled children.

"Hi, Bob, you ready for the trip?" asked Neville, as Bob climbed into the passenger seat.

"Sure am," said Bob, taking his sunglasses out of his pocket and putting them on. "I'm really looking forward to getting out of the city and seeing some more of the countryside."

They wound their way up several small streets to the Belcan Bridge that took them over to Central American Boulevard, which, though it was the city's widest street, would hardly qualify as a grand Latin American-style boulevard. Turning right on Cemetery Road, which bisected the cemetery, they found themselves blocked by a funeral procession. Led by a man in a black suit and a homburg playing a sad tune on a coronet, the mourners, carrying parasols, slowly walked along behind a horse-drawn hearse. Traffic waited patiently until they left the road headed for an open grave. Only then could Bob and Neville resume their journey, leaving the cemetery behind, and progressing though a landfill site that sent a powerful odor of rotting garbage into Bob's overly sensitive American nostrils.

"I hate to have to say this, Bob," Neville said as the car accelerated. "But I hear you've been seen in the company of Mr. Nick Devlin. I'm sure you don't know much about him. But if I were you, I'd steer clear of him."

"Why? What do you know about him?"

"Nothing really for sure, just rumors. I can't tell you anything specific, but I do hear that some of his associates are pretty rough characters."

"Well, he seems okay to me. He's just a businessman, you know."

"So he says, but I doubt it," said Neville, as the Toyota slowed for a speed bump, or sleeping policeman as they're called in Belize.

The trip to Belmopan on the Western Highway was only about fifty miles and took an hour. The road first went west along the mangrove-covered coast, as Belize City was built on a delta that projected out into the sea. Then the road continued inland in a westerly direction.

On the way out of town, a prominent sign put up by the National Aids Prevention and Control Program colorfully warned, "If you wa mek love, wear a glove." As they got further inland, they reached Hattieville, a town, which Neville told Bob, was founded on high ground after residents of Belize City took refuge there from Hurricane Hattie in 1961. The road had been cut through a thick tropical forest treed with palms and hardwoods. A few clapboard homesteads with tin roofs lined the road. Occasionally, Zebu cattle with their big humps, dewlaps and floppy ears could be seen grazing in the scrub fields along the road. Vultures, or Johnny Crows as they are called in Belize, circled lazily overhead looking for a nice flattened iguana or some other tasty morsel of roadkill to eat. Every once in a while, they passed the remains of an abandoned car. If a car broke down and it was too old to be worth fixing, the local custom, evidently dictated by economics and not ecology, was to push it in the ditch. While this didn't do much to beautify the landscape, it obviously was a lot cheaper than having the wreck towed back to Belize City.

At mile 32 on the Western Highway, they stopped for gas at JB's Watering Hole, a place that with some justification billed itself as being "in the middle of nowhere." JB's had been especially popular with the British soldiers that used to be stationed in Belize. Bob saw their many regimental banners hanging from the roof and walls on his way to the bathroom. Unfortunately, it was too early to sample some of the fine beer that kept so many young Brits happily hydrated in the hot tropical sun.

Back on the road, it wasn't long before they could see the rocky Mayan Mountains in the distance off on the left. Projecting like dragon teeth from the flat terrain, these unusually shaped mountains gave the landscape a starkly beautiful and surreal air.

The sky darkened. Soon a tropical storm caught them from behind. The rain came down so hard that the windshield wipers could not clear the front windshields. Neville pulled over to the side of the road.

"We're gonna have to wait this one out," he said.

"It's unbelievable," said Bob. "Just like someone opened a floodgate above in the sky."

Within five minutes, the rain had let up enough that they were able to continue on their way. The rain turned to a light drizzle, and a rainbow appeared over the mountains. The volatility of the weather made the landscape even more spectacular.

By the time they got to the crossroads near Belmopan, the rain had stopped entirely. Neville turned off the Western Highway, slowed for another sleeping policeman, and drove into town. He apologized to Bob for the plainness and sleepiness of the country's capital.

"The government moved here after the hurricane. But everything else stayed in Belize City. It's getting better, though. With the growth of the government and the influx of refugees from Central America, the population is now over ten thousand. And there are finally at least a few stores, including a small Brodie's department store, and a couple of restaurants," he said, beginning to give Bob the five-minute tour as they took the Ring Road around the town. "That's the market square over there where all the buses stop. You can see the carts selling food and other local crafts. And that building on the hill with the flag that looks a little like a Mayan pyramid is the National Assembly. Those buildings around it are government offices."

They pulled off the road on the shoulder in front of the Bull Frog Inn, a small roadside hotel with twenty-five rooms that represented the height of luxury in Belmopan. "This is where you'll be staying for the next few days while you work. It's not too bad and the food is pretty good if you like rice and beans," Neville laughed.

After Bob checked in and dropped his bags in the room, they met in the large tropical-style dining room, which extended outside onto a terrace. Following a lunch of escabeche, a tangy Belizean soup made of chicken and onions, Neville took Bob over to their office. It was in a room in a small house on Unity Boulevard, a couple of blocks from the hotel, where the man lived who administered the project on a part-time basis. They knocked on the door and a small Hispanic woman with Indian features opened the door.

"Buenas dias, Neville," she said. "We've been expecting you. Alejandro will be back from work around four, but you can go right in to the office."

"Gracias, Conchita. Señor Wayne is anxious to get to work," said Neville, taking Bob down the hall to a little room. Inside were boxes of receipts and piles of paper everywhere, even on top of the computer.

"You can see I wasn't lying when I told you that it's a real mess," said Neville. "You still think you can clean it up by the weekend?"

"I'll try," groaned Bob, seeing that he may have bitten off more than he could chew.

"Good, then give me a call when you're done and I'll come back up from Belize City and pick you up," Neville said cheerfully, going out the door, glad to have transferred ownership of the Rotary Club's accounting problem over to Bob.

For the next five days, Bob spent ten hours a day in that little stuffy hot room transforming all those messy piles of paper into coherent financial statements for the past five years. The task was not totally overwhelming, but it came close. Conchita, who was very nice, but spoke little English, kept him well fueled with coffee. Alejandro, a short, plump, dapper man with a big mustache, who was supposed to be the project administrator, wasn't much help. In fact, he seemed to be so embarrassed by the state of the books that he made himself scarce when Bob was around. It was just as well. Bob wasn't very sympathetic. How could Alejandro let it get so out of hand? he asked, giving full rein to the self-satisfied feeling of superiority that came over accountants at such moments.

Determined to see the job through, Bob attacked it with the single-minded tenacity for which his profession is renowned. After all, wasn't that the reason why I had told Donna I was coming down here? he asked himself. In some strange way, the work seemed to assuage his feeling of guilt for leaving Donna. It was an accountant's way of doing penance.

In the week that Bob stayed in Belmopan, the high point of his day was in the evening when he systematically sampled the Bullfrog's extensive menu. Steak with rice and beans and fried plantain, roast chicken with rice and beans and fried plantain, and pork chop with, of course, rice and beans and fried plantain. Bob enjoyed the meat, which was raised by local Mennonites and was all of excellent quality, even if he didn't share the Belizean insatiable craving for rice and beans and fried plantain.

One night Bob had the opportunity to try stewed gibnut, an unusual local delicacy, with his rice and beans and fried plantain. Eating gibnut has become something of an initiation right for foreigners visiting Belize. When Queen Elizabeth tried it on her trip to Belize, one of the British tabloids reported "QUEEN EATS RAT IN BELIZE." Since then the large brown-spotted rodent with a gamey taste has been dignified with the title of the Royal Gibnut, not in Burke's Peerage, of course, but unofficially.

In the long, hot tropical nights after dinner, Bob became drinking buddies with Jimmy Bullfrog, as the scion of the Spanish family that ran the hotel was affectionately called. Jimmy introduced him to many of the regulars that frequented the Bullfrog—government ministers, public servants, ambassadors, planters and local business people. This was the local elite who inhabited a totally different world from the Central American refugees who lived in the settlement right across the road from the hotel.

One day at lunch, the old lady, Jimmy's mother, the Grande Dame of the Bullfrog family herself, took Bob on a tour of the private orchid and bromeliad garden on the property. On Mariachi night, which was on Tuesdays, Bob lingered after dinner to watch the locals who came to dance to Mexican music. On Wednesday night, he saw a Mennonite couple drive up to the hotel in a horse-drawn buggy to have dinner. All this made him think of Donna, his trailer park princess, as he used to teasingly call her. I really should give her a call when I get back to Belize City, he thought.

On Thursday night, a disheveled American wearing a cowboy hat and boots and a belt with a big silver buckle came into the Bullfrog in a very agitated state and waving a gun. He'd been drinking and was mumbling something about an argument and shooting somebody who was trespassing on his citrus farm down the Hummingbird Highway. A little later the police arrived and led the man meekly away. All the while, everyone continued to eat rice and beans and fried plantain. Just another peaceful night at the Bullfrog.

By Saturday morning, when all the work was over, Bob was glad to see Neville when he returned to pick him up. Before returning to Belize City, they were going to drive out to San José Succotz to see Pedro Uck, the young Mayan teacher who had been helped by the Rotary project. He was going to show them around Xunantunich, the nearby ruins of a Mayan city. Bob was anxious to get out and do something more active after days of piecing together badly-organized books and hanging around the Bullfrog eating enough rice and beans to turn him into a Belizean.

"I brought you a little present as a token of our appreciation," said Neville once they were in the car. "It will help you to understand where we're going and what we're going to see. It's on the back seat."

Picking up the book, Bob read from the cover, "*The Maya of Belize* by Simon Butterfield. Hey! I know him. I met him at Lamanai. He was a really nice fellow."

"Yes," said Neville. "And he's written one of the most readable travel books about the Mayans. I'm sure you'll enjoy it if you're at all interested in learning more about them."

"I sure am," said Bob. "Is there anything in it about the jade head?"

"Of course," said Neville. "Everybody is interested in the jade head. You'll find the whole story—that is, at least everything we know."

San José Succotz is a small Mayan village situated in the lush Mopan Valley, just south of the Western Highway, about thirty miles west of Belmopan. Spread out around a central green are small houses made of wood and cinder block with corrugated tin roofs intermixed with the occasional traditional thatch hut. The houses are separated by small gardens of corn and other vegetables, and shaded by banana, breadfruit and mango trees, and cohune palms. One of the village structures houses a store where traditional Mayan handicrafts are offered for sale.

Pedro's house was one of the more modern ones on the road coming into the village, but it was very small as he lived alone. When they drove up, Pedro was sitting in a chair on the front porch reading a book. Seeing them, he got up and came out to the vehicle. A handsome young man of medium height who walked with a slight limp, he had a smooth olive complexion and shiny black hair.

"Welcome to my village," he said, extending his hand to greet the two men.

"Thank you," said Neville. "You're really getting around well now. You know, I haven't seen you since right after you got back from the Shriner's Hospital in the States. It must have been eight years ago now."

"Yes, while it's hard to believe, it was that long ago. It took me a while to get used to my artificial leg. But I can do everything now except play soccer. I'm really thankful to the Rotary for helping me to walk again. It's given me a chance to live a normal life."

"I'm pleased to hear that. It's good to meet someone who has been helped so much by our program. It makes our efforts worthwhile," said Bob, feeling proud and glad to be reminded that some good will come out of the unpleasant week he had spent in Belmopan in the small room with all those musty smelling receipts.

"Come on, Pedro" said Neville. "I'm anxious to go see the ruins again. And I hear you're one of the best guides around."

"Yes, of course, it was my Mayan ancestors who built the temple in the first place. I take all my primary school students up to see it every year so they can better understand our heritage."

The three men got back in the SUV and drove down the hill towards the river to the ferry landing. The ferryman with his straw hat in his hand motioned for them to drive right onto the old two-car ferry. A few

Mayans who were walking along also scurried to get on the boat. Once on the ferry, Bob, Neville and Pedro got out of the SUV and stood along the rail as the ferryman turned a hand crank attached to a cable that pulled them slowly across the river. On the rocks in the rapids up the river, Mayan women could be seen brightly dressed in *huipils,* doing their laundry while their children swam in the river, as their people had done for thousands of years. The deep pool that the ferry crossed was surrounded by overhanging tree branches. After the five minutes it took to get to the other side of the river, the three men got back in the car. The Mayans disembarked first and went off down a forest path to their cornfields. Neville drove the SUV off the ferry and they started up a steep hill to the ruins. Huge palms arched over the mile-long track, which was cut through the dense jungle like a tunnel.

At the summit of the hill, they parked their car in a rocky clearing and walked up over the crest into the courtyard surrounded by long mounds with masonry work on top. The high-pitched calls of birds could be heard coming from the bush, and yellow and blue butterflies fluttered back and forth across the clearing. At the far end of the plaza, perched on the limestone cliff that towered over the Mopan River Valley, stood the spectacular El Castillo or Castle.

"Xunantunich is a classic period ceremonial center that thrived from about 150 AD to 850 AD," said Pedro. "It means 'stone maiden' in Mayan. This is a recent name, not the original one, which has been lost in the mists of time. The story is that a local Mayan, who was out hunting in the ruins, was suddenly brought to a state of sexual arousal by the sight of a beautiful, statuesque maiden who was glowing white in the rays of the rising sun. The 'stone' part of the name comes from what was said to be her stony gaze across the valley to the site of what is now Succotz, our village.

"Unfortunately, I can't tell you much of the real history of Xunantunich. There's never been a systematic large-scale excavation of the site. And its proximity to the highway has brought many looters who have removed or destroyed significant finds that might have told us something about the site's history. At least now, though, the site's finally protected. Under Belize law all 'ancient monuments' and 'antiquities' are the property of the state and can't be removed and sold. Needless to say, though, that doesn't stop some people," said Pedro, the increasing loudness of his voice revealing his outrage at the looters of his heritage.

"How do they get the artifacts out of the country?" asked Bob, with his usual insensitivity.

"Some people fly them out in private planes," replied Neville, who was less personally attached to the country's Mayan heritage and thus less hostile to the activities of looters. "But most people just take them in their luggage. The rarest and most valuable objects are jade or gold and can fit in a carry-on."

"Oh," said Bob. "I see."

"Let's go take a look at the stelae the archeologists found here," said Pedro. "They will give you a better appreciation of the age of the place."

Under the thatched shelter in front of El Castillo lay three stelae on their backs. On two of them, there were Mayan numbers, which had not been eroded by the elements and could still be decoded. For the uninitiated, Mayan numbers are base twenty and are represented in two ways. The first, called normal form glyphs, depict numbers similar to the way Roman numerals do by bars (▌) for fives, dots (•) for ones, and combinations for the other numbers. However, the Mayans were more advanced and also had the concept of zero, which was depicted by a shell symbol. Another exception is twenty which is represented by a dot above a shell. The second way of indicating numbers is called portrait glyphs. It represents numbers by the heads of different gods.

The first stelae was inscribed 10 . 0. 0. 0. 0 or

The second read:

"The first stelae bears the date of the beginning of the tenth baktun, or 830 AD by your calendar," said Pedro. "That marked the beginning of the period of one of the death gods and signaled the beginning of the end of Classic Mayan civilization. The second stelae bears the date of the end of the first katun or twenty year period of the tenth baktun. It's one of the last dated stelae in the Mayan world and certainly the last one from Xunantunich."

"Dr. Butterfield at Lamanai told me a bit about the decline of Mayan civilization," said Bob. "It's all very mysterious."

"Yes, it is," affirmed Pedro. "But enough talk. Let's climb to the top of El Castillo and take a look."

"Can you climb it?" asked Neville, wondering if Pedro could make the demanding climb with his prosthesis."Sure," said Pedro. "Just watch me!"

They walked to the other end of the plaza and started the 130-foot climb to the top, first going up the terraced stairs on the front side and then circling around to the back. As they climbed, Bob and Neville quickly tired and had to rest a few times. Pedro indulged them, although, buoyed by the strength of youth, he really had no need to stop. Halfway up on the eastern side of the tower, they saw a frieze adorned by the Mayan glyphs for the sun, moon, Venus and different days. The frieze also had the image of a headless man.

"The headless man might have been a local chieftain who was beheaded for rebelling against the formidable lords of Xunantunich," speculated Pedro.

At the top of the tower was a corbel-vaulted temple built on the rubble of earlier temples. From the top, Pedro proudly pointed out the site's three plazas below, before taking them around to the backside to show them why this place was so special to the Maya. There, from a height of more than four hundred feet, could be seen a breathtaking view of the Mopan River Valley. It took in the mestizo town of Benque Viejo below and extended all the way to Guatemala. Xunantunich was definitely a place Bob would never forget.

15

The Wal-Mart, which was a new mega-store at the northern end of the great strip mall that grew like a cancer northward out of the town, was the new commercial heart of Loganville. Its establishment had sounded the death knell of many of the town's venerable old family-owned retail stores. Survival of the fittest it's called. It's the way capitalism works. The townspeople, as much as they mourned the loss of local businesses, still voted with their pocketbooks for the greater variety and selection offered by the great commercial juggernaut. But this didn't stop them from nostalgically lamenting the decay of the old downtown and longing for the old-fashioned simpler world it represented.

Donna and Connie joined the crowd at Wal-Mart that Saturday morning as they happily chatted and pushed their cart down the aisle in the cosmetic section. So far, they had bought shampoo, hair dye, blush, lipstick and mascara, but the shopping had not been easy. It had required elaborate and animated discussions about the merits of each product as they carefully compared their features and price before deciding which one of the many seemingly identical products to put in the cart. They were now on their way over to the women's clothing section to get some clothes for Donna to wear at her new job.

"How do you like working at Gallagher's?" Connie asked.

"It pays the bills, but it's pretty hard being on my feet for so long. The high heels I have to wear give me blisters and cause my legs and back to hurt."

"Can't you wear flats?"

"No, it's part of the uniform like the white blouses and black skirt I need to get. Hey, these blouses look okay, don't they? They're mediums. They should fit."

"Sure. How late do you have to work?"

" 'Til two in the morning. That's another..."

"SPECIAL ON ONEIDA FLATWARE IN THE HOUSEWARES DEPARTMENT," blared over the loudspeaker, interrupting Donna and causing her to pause in mid-sentence before continuing.

"...bad thing. I don't like leaving Sarah alone so late at night."

"She's a good kid. She won't get in any trouble."

"I'm not so sure about that. You should've seen the guy I threw out of the house several weeks ago. They were smoking pot together and he looked like he belonged to the Hell's Angels."

"We all tried a little pot when we were in high school. It didn't hurt us, did it? I wouldn't make too much of it, if I were you."

"It's easy for you to say. She's not your daughter. It sure worries the hell out of me, particularly after that boy overdosed a couple of weeks ago at the party over on Elmwood Drive. Sarah or Jessica could easily have been there."

"Yeah, I guess you're right," said Connie. "It is worrying the way there are so many more hard drugs around these days. I caught Jessica smoking marijuana on the back porch last year. I gave her a stern lecture. I think she's stopped, though. She hangs out with a pretty good group of kids."

"Exactly, that's my worry about Sarah. That she'll fall in with the wrong crowd like that motorcycle guy."

Donna browsed through the skirt rack until she found the black skirts. "Here's a size six. It should fit. Excuse me a minute. I'm gonna go back in the dressing room to try things on."

A couple of minutes later Donna came out with the blouses and skirt over her arm.

"How did they fit?" asked Connie.

"Perfect, I'm still a perfect six," said Donna curtseying to Connie. "It sure will be good to have a change of clothes. I was really getting tired of having to wash my one blouse and skirt every day before going to work."

On their way to the cashier, Connie just had to ask, "Heard anything from Bob?"

"Not for a couple of weeks, but I'm sure he'll call again soon. There must be some kind of problem with the phones down there."

"Right! I'm not gonna say any more. You already know my views on Bob," said Connie.

"Will that be cash or charge?" said a smiling African-American girl in a blue Wal-Mart smock.

"Charge," said Donna, giving the girl her Visa card.

The girl put the clothes and cosmetics in a bag and gave Donna the receipt to sign. Then Connie similarly paid for her cosmetics with plastic.

On the way out, Connie said, "You could get a job as an 'Associate' here too if you wanted. The pay would probably be better than Gallagher's and you'd get some benefits."

"Yeah, but it's the tips that make the difference. When the guys get drinking, they get pretty loose with their money as long as they like your looks. I think I've got a few more years left," said Donna, sucking in her stomach and sticking out her breasts.

"What you really mean is as long as they like your tits," joked Connie.

"You said it, not me," laughed Donna.

The Riverview Manor was a retirement home for the elderly, not the town's more affluent seniors who lived at the Logan Estates up by the lake, but the ordinary people who had worked hard their whole life and had little left to show for it. These people were forced to rely on government subsidized housing in their declining years. Donna had come out for the afternoon to do the hair of a couple of the residents. One of the utility rooms with a sink had been transformed into a makeshift beauty parlor by the addition of a hair dryer someone had donated. Supplies of shampoos, hair dyes, and curlers were on the floor in a box that had been retrieved from the storage closet. A big mirror hung on the wall behind the sink. One of the residents, Mrs. Farlow, was sitting in the chair in front of the sink. Dressed in a stained pale blue cover-up and wearing green rubber gloves, Donna had finished giving her a shampoo and was working some Miss Clairol Nice and Easy Light Chestnut Brown hair dye into her almost entirely grey head.

"This will make you look twenty years younger," Donna said.

"I wish my husband, Orville, was still around to see, but he's been gone for almost ten years now," said Mrs. Farlow.

"I'm sure there are other men around here who will appreciate it."

"Oh, child, I'm too old for that. But it sure is nice for you to come out here, though. The girls really look forward to it."

"I started coming out here with my mother to visit my grandmother a couple of years back. I used to do her hair. Some of the other women asked me if I would do theirs, too. When grannie died, I just kept on coming out."

"Your grandmother had already passed away when my children put me in here, but I'd seen her a few times around town over the years. Her husband was a farmer, wasn't he?" inquired Mrs. Farlow.

"Yeah, they had a small spread downstream on the Green Fork River. When gramps died, she tried to stay on the farm, but, after a few years, it was too much for her. So she sold it and bought a little bungalow in town. When she couldn't take care of herself any more, we had to move her in here. She didn't like it very much at first, but there wasn't really any choice. Eventually, though, she made a few friends and got to like it better."

"What ever happened to your mother and father?" asked Mrs. Farlow.

"Oh, Mom still lives in town, but Dad died a few years back."

"Oh, yes, I'd heard about that. It was a terrible accident when the grain elevator exploded."

"Yeah, it was awful, but it worked out okay for Mom. The settlement she got was enough to buy the new ranch-style house she had always wanted. It's funny, if Dad had lived, they'd have been broke and still living in the trailer park out in Hungry Hollow. He never saved a nickel and would've had to live on social security. "

"You see her often?" asked Mrs. Farlow.

"Yeah, every couple of days, and of course we speak on the phone every day."

"How's Bob?"

"Oh, he's okay. He's away for a while...er...on a vacation, but I hope he'll be back soon."

Donna rinsed the dye out of Mrs. Farlow's hair and put curlers in. Mrs. Farlow then went to sit under the dryer. Ten minutes later, when her hair was dry, she moved back into the other chair so that Donna could take out the curlers and style her hair. After Donna had finished, she held up a hand mirror.

"Whaddaya think?" Donna asked.

"Don't I look bea-uuu-tiful!" laughed Mrs. Farlow.

The ringing of the telephone woke Donna from a deep sleep. She looked at her clock and saw that it was only eight-thirty in the morning. The alarm wasn't set to ring for another hour and a half. She had worked a full shift at Gallagher's the night before and hadn't planned on getting up before ten. She reached drowsily for the telephone on the night table next to her bed, hoping it would be Bob.

"Hello," she said into the telephone receiver.

"Hello, Mrs. Blake, I'm Mrs. Tilton, Sarah's English teacher at Loganville High School. I'd like to talk to you about Sarah."

"What about Sarah?" Donna asked, her heart bearing faster. "Is there something wrong?"

"Well, she wasn't in my class yesterday afternoon. She missed two classes last week, too. Her performance has been falling as well. She didn't hand in her essay last week and her journal is not up to date. I'm afraid that if we had to give out report cards today, she wouldn't pass the course."

"What do you think's the problem?" asked Donna, becoming even more concerned.

"I don't know," said Mrs. Tilton. "She's always very polite and not a behavioral problem in class. And she always used to do satisfactory work."

"I'll have to talk to her. I'd appreciate it if you could let me know right away if she misses any more classes."

"Certainly, I'd be glad to."

"Okay, thanks for calling."

"You're welcome. Bye."

"Bye."

What the devil is Sarah up to? thought Donna. I'll have to get to the bottom of this. And quick!

Later that afternoon when Sarah came home from school, she found her mother sitting in the dining room drinking a coffee and reading the *Loganville Gazette.*

"I got a call from Mrs. Tilton at the school today," Donna said.

"So," replied Sarah.

"She tells me you haven't been coming to English class and that you're on the way to failing. What have you got to say for yourself?"

"Nuttin'."

"You can do better than that."

"Whaddaya mean?"

"I mean, have you been skipping school to hang out with that motorcycle guy?"

"Well, ...not really."

"What do you mean, not really?"

"Well, I have seen him, but we haven't really been hanging out together."

"How's that?"

"I've gone over to the Loganville Jail to visit him a couple of times during visiting hours. He's being held in custody. But I wouldn't call that 'hanging out'."

"In jail! Don't tell me. It's for drug dealing."

"Well, yeah, but he told me he didn't do it."

"Right! That's what they all say."

"No, Mom, really, the police put fifty grams of cocaine and a gun in his motorcycle saddle bags to frame him. He wouldn't lie to me."

"Sure they did! I don't care what he says. I don't want you seeing him anymore."

Sarah didn't reply. Her passive resistance worried Donna, but she consoled herself with the thought that, from the sounds of it, this young hooligan was likely to do some serious time. She'd have plenty of time to try to wean Sarah from him. Maybe Bob could help when he got back, that is, she was beginning to wonder, if he came back.

16

Bob was glad to be back in Belize City again. After Belmopan, it seemed like civilization. He was welcomed as a long-lost friend at the weekly Rotary Club meeting at the Fort George Hotel where he briefly reported on his work in Belmopan. The members listened politely, although the topic was dreary. Bob liked the sense of belonging that he got from socializing with his fellow Rotarians. He was also getting to feel more comfortable in the town. No longer intimidated by the local panhandlers and street people, he enjoyed walking around and observing the rich mix of Caribbean and Central American culture that made the streets so lively. One day he took a long walk down Albert Street to St. John's Anglican Cathedral.

St. John's is an impressive brick structure with arched Georgian-style windows which was built in 1820 by slaves using bricks brought over from England as ballast in the hulls of ships. Four Mosquito Kings were crowned in the cathedral. They were the ones who ruled over the Mosquito Indians that inhabited Nicaragua's Mosquito Coast and maintained close ties with the British.

On a whim, Bob went inside the church. Plaques commemorating early parishioners hung from the walls. He sat down in one of the pews at the back of the church. It was the first time he'd been in a real church since his first wedding. The silence and solitude made him feel at peace with himself and the universe. It didn't last long, though, as his thoughts soon turned to the many failures and disappointments in his life—his failed marriages, his strained relationships with his oldest sons Alan and Matt, no job, no money, and the creditors waiting to hound him when he returned home. He wished he could make a new, fresh start. If only he had something to start with. What could he do? He sat for the better part of an hour before coming to the obvious conclusion that it wouldn't do him any good to keep obsessing over the same problems. Time to go back to the outside world, he thought. As he left, he hoped to leave his many troubles behind him in this place of contemplation, a strategy Ernest Hemingway never tried.

When Bob got back to the guest house, he was greeted at the door by an agitated Elsa.

"Mr. Wayne, Mr. Wayne, somebody broke into your room while you were out," gasped Elsa, all out of breath. "This hasn't ever happened here before. No, never. You know, this is a very respectable house, Mr. Wayne. I just stepped out for a few minutes to get some groceries. And when I got back, I found the door to your room open and your bag and drawers all dumped out on the floor."

"Calm down, Elsa," said Bob, trying to be reassuring to cover up his own alarm. "Let's go up and take a look."

Stepping into the hall, Bob went up the stairs two at a time, leaving Elsa to waddle up behind him. When he got into his room, he went directly over to his suitcase to check the secret pocket where he hid his valuables. "Oh, no!" he said, "my money is gone. All I've got now is what's left in my wallet." He rummaged desperately around on the floor under all the clothes in a vain attempt to find his money. But all he came up with was his plane ticket and his passport under a crumpled-up shirt. "At least I haven't lost everything," he said, looking up at Elsa who had finally made it up the stairs.

"You'll have to go down to the Police Station and report this, Mr. Wayne," Elsa said.

"Yeah, I will later this afternoon," Bob said. But by the look on his face, Elsa could see that he didn't have much hope and just wanted to be left alone.

"I'm going back downstairs, Mr. Wayne. If there's anything I can do, just call."

"Thanks, Elsa," said Bob, who was staring disconsolately at all his stuff spread all over the floor.

After Bob had recovered enough to pick up all his belongings and put them back in the suitcase or drawers out of which they had been ripped, he trudged down the stairs and walked dutifully over to the Police Station. It was only a few blocks away at the corner of Queen St. and New Road. Entering the main office through the front door, he went right over to the counter and reported the robbery to the policeman on duty. The uniformed man filled out the required form as Bob gave him the details.

"How much money did you say was missing?" the policeman said, scratching his bald head, which was ringed with a fringe of woolly gray hair.

"I guess about $1,600," Bob answered.

"Wow! That's a lot of cash to leave lying around in a hotel room," the policeman said. "Couldn't you have put it somewhere for safekeeping?"

"Yes, I guess I could have. Elsa had a small safe in her office," replied Bob.

"Well, I'm afraid I can't hold out much hope that you'll get your money back, since we don't really have much to go on."

"Yeah, I figured as much, but Elsa wanted me to report it anyway," said Bob. "She was very upset to have a robbery in her guest house."

"Yes, she's never had one before. It's strange, but you're the first. Well, Mr. Wayne, we'll do our best. I'm sorry your vacation had to be spoiled in this way."

"Thanks," said Bob, getting up to leave.

Going out the front door of the Police Station, Bob could see that it was almost five o'clock from the small picturesque clock tower in the middle of the road. He turned and retraced his steps back to Elsa's. When he arrived, there was a message waiting for him. It was from Nick asking Bob to meet him at the Fort Street Restaurant for dinner at seven o'clock. He guessed he'd better go. He had been counting on the money he had won at the casino to keep him going a few more weeks and now it was gone. Nick had asked him to do some work earlier. It looked like he would have to take it now whether he liked it or not, that is, if it were still available. He had no choice now, but to put his misgivings aside and to go and find out what it was.

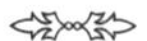

The Fort Street Restaurant was only a few blocks from Elsa's. Since it used to be a small private hospital, it had much larger grounds than most homes in the Fort George district. Bob went through the gate and walked up the long gravel walk. When he got to the impressive green staircase, he took it up to the second floor verandah. Like many old buildings in Belize City, the ground floor was not used for living space because of the danger posed by flooding for a town only a couple of feet above sea level. Inside, he looked around and saw Nick sitting at a candle-lit table near the window, smoking a Cuban cigar and sipping a Scotch on the rocks. Bob went over to join him.

"Hello, Nick, it's good to see you again. I'd been meaning to give you a call," said Bob, shaking Nick's hand before taking his seat.

"I couldn't wait," said Nick. "You remember I offered you a little accounting job the last time we met and you never gave me an answer."

"Yes, I'm sorry. I meant to. But I got kinda busy. And you wouldn't believe what happened to me today."

"What?" asked Nick, looking totally unconcerned.

"My hotel room was robbed and I lost most of the money I had left from my winnings the time you took me to the casino," said Bob.

"Well, I'm sorry, but maybe that will help you make up your mind about the job I have for you."

"Whaddaya want me to do?" asked Bob.

"I want you to take the manual accounting system we have for our various businesses up at the plantation and convert it to the QuickBooks computerized accounting program."

"That's an easy job. Why don't you get one of the local accountants to do it?"

"That's just what I don't want. As I told you before, nothing stays confidential down here for very long. Everybody knows everybody else and they all talk."

"You don't have much faith in accountants. You know we're bound by the code of our profession to keep our clients' business confidential."

"Don't give me all that crap about professional ethics. It's not accountants I don't trust. It's people," said Nick, exhaling a puff of cigar smoke.

"Why trust me?"

"Who said I trusted you? You're an outsider who's only down here for a few months. Once you're gone, there will be no one around to talk about my business. Get the picture?"

"Yep."

"Well, willya do it or not?"

"I guess I'll have to since most of my money's gone and I'm not quite ready to go home yet. How much will you pay me?"

"How does ten thousand dollars sound?"

"Very generous!" said Bob enthusiastically, as it was much more than he'd expected. It would make up for the stolen money and give him some extra to boot. His luck was starting to turn again.

"I'll have Jules come around tomorrow and pick you up and take you out to the plantation. It's up toward Orange Walk Town off the Northern Highway about fifty miles northwest of here."

"Okay, deal," said Bob, reaching across the table to shake Nick's hand and seal the arrangement.

"Miss," Nick said in a commanding voice to a passing waitress who was on her way to another table with a tray of food. "Can you bring us some menus right away. We'd like to order and we don't have all night.

After dinner that night, Nick took Bob to the Paradise Club. It was in a gated estate on the outskirts of town. When they arrived in the SUV, the security guard saw Nick in the back seat and motioned them through with a wave of his hand. Once inside the mansion, which housed the club, it looked like an ordinary bar except more garish. The lounge was decorated with heavy red velvet curtains and gold filigreed red wallpaper and an elaborate cut-glass chandelier. The chairs and couches were crude takeoffs of Louis XIV style, painted antique white, with red cushions. The tables had white marble tops. There were four or five other guests, all men. They were a mixed-race group all casually dressed, but quite prosperous looking. Bob remarked that one of them was the same Creole man who had been at their table playing high-stakes poker at the Princess Casino. Another was a middle-aged man who was dressed in khakis and had a full grey beard that made him look like Papa Hemingway. A host dressed in a white dinner jacket and bow tie greeted Nick and Bob and took them over to a table in the corner. Nick sprawled out on the couch in the corner, leaving Bob to sit in the armchair.

The waiter came and Bob ordered another planter's punch. This made his sixth for the night. He was well launched and feeling no pain. Nick had another Scotch. Drink didn't seem to affect him like it did Bob. Becoming progressively more gregarious the more he drank, Bob spilled out the sad tale of his disappointing life. Nick didn't say too much of anything, but lent him what, at least to Bob in his semi-stupefied state, seemed to be a sympathetic ear.

After a while, Bob asked, "Why did you bring me all the way out here to drink? We could've drunk in town."

"You'll see in a little while that this place has a lot more to offer," said Nick.

After another couple of drinks, as Bob was measuring time that night in glasses instead of coffee spoons, about ten young women came in through the back door—a few were Creole, some Hispanic, and others white. They were all heavily made up and looked like extras from the cast of *Moulin Rouge.* They began to circulate flirtatiously among the guests, provocatively positioning themselves on the furniture as they went.

"Do you prefer chocolate, vanilla, or coffee?" asked Nick.

Recognizing that Nick was not talking about his choice of beverage, Bob stammered something unintelligible. It was not that he was a prude, but this definitely was not what he was expecting and he felt very uncomfortable. Sure, he'd had casual sex, but he'd never paid for it. And it had always been when he'd drunk too much alcohol and he'd always regretted it afterwards.

"Well, if you won't choose, I'll pick a variety," said Nick motioning to three of the girls to join them in the booth. A tall thin Creole woman with dyed reddish hair, a black-haired Latina woman, and a blonde with an Eastern European accent came over. The blonde sat on Bob's lap in the armchair and rubbed his ears, his face turning brighter red with each caress. The two dark-haired women sat down on each side of Nick on the couch and draped their arms around him.

"How's this?" Nick asked. "How about some drinks for the girls," he shouted to the waiter.

Three drinks came quickly. Nick and his two girls were laughing and flirting. Bob knew he was in over his head, but didn't know quite what to do. Through an alcoholic haze, he could hear the blonde Nick had assigned to him trying to make small talk.

"What's your name, handsome?" she asked.

"Bob," he said.

"Mine's Lara. Where're you from?"

"The United States."

"That's where I'm gonna move as soon as I get enough money," she said.

"Let's go upstairs for a while," said Nick, sweeping up his two girls in his arms and heading up the staircase, like a movie producer herding starlets.

Bob felt dizzy when he stood up. But by hanging onto Lara, he managed to make it up the stairs. Nick and the girls went into the first room on the left. Lara took him to the room at the end of the hall. It had a big double bed with a red silk bedspread and curtains and faux Louis XIV furniture like that downstairs. A bowl filled with condoms sat on the bedside table. Lara sat him down on the bed and went into the bathroom. He could hear the shower running. When she came back, she was wearing a sheer black negligee."How do I look?" she asked, turning around for him to admire her from all angles.

"Good," stammered Bob nervously. "You look good."

"Before we get started, it's your turn," she said, motioning toward the bathroom.

"No...no...I'd rather not," he said.

"But the management insists on cleanliness. It's our policy," she said.

"I don't feel very well," he said.

"What's wrong, sweetie?" she said. "Afraid you won't be able to get it up?"

"I don't know. I've been drinking a lot."

"Let me rub you a bit. That always helps," she said kneeling on the floor in front of him and starting to massage his groin through his pants.

"No, please, I'd rather you didn't do that," he said, pushing her away.

"Okay, whatever," she said, getting a little bit put off. "You know it's on Nick's tab. It won't cost you anything."

"I'm not surprised to hear that. Speaking of Nick, I wouldn't want him to think, ...well, you know. If I gave you an extra forty dollars, say? Would you promise not to say anything to him?"

"Sure, sugar, anything you say," she said, her mood lightening.

They went back downstairs and had another drink while they waited for Nick.

"How did you end up here?" asked Bob, indulging his masculine curiosity about what could lead a woman to become a prostitute.

"I saw an ad back home in the Ukraine in the paper and I needed the money. I have a young son to feed and didn't have a job."

"Did you bring him along?"

"No, no, I couldn't. He's back home with his grandmother. I send them money to live."

"Oh, I see," said Bob, starting to see her more sympathetically as a real person with problems of her own, beside which his own paled. Bob and Lara made small talk for about an hour before Nick finally came down the stairs, as he went up, with an arm around each of the two girls. He laughed to see Bob already downstairs.

"What's wrong? Did you fizzle out?" he ribbed, pointing his finger out and then letting it droop down suggestively.

"No, no, everything was okay," replied Bob defensively.

"You should try an Oreo sandwich next time," Nick said.

Bob was too embarrassed to reply.

It was well after midnight when they finally left the club. As he got up, Bob looked at Lara and put his finger up to his lips. She nodded her agreement. In the parking lot, Bob and Nick found Jules fast asleep in the driver's seat. Nick opened the door and shook him roughly.

"Wake up, c'mon, we're ready to go," he said.

"Okay, Boss, okay," replied a groggy Jules.

Bob and Nick climbed into the back seat. The car lurched backwards out of the parking spot. There was a muffled thud and then a bump as if the car had hit something. Nick got out to see what was the matter. There laying on the ground, covered in blood, was the Creole man from the Princess Casino, his gold chain still around his neck. Perhaps he had been staggering out to his car and passed out in the parking lot on the ground behind Nick's car—definitely not a good place to sleep it off. Or maybe somebody had knocked him out and stuck him behind Nick's car on purpose. Who knows? Who cares? Certainly not Nick. He was already climbing back in the car.

"What was it, Nick?" asked Bob.

"Oh, nothing," said Nick, brushing Bob's question aside. "Let's go, Jules. Step on it. I'm anxious to get home."

Taking Nick at his word, Jules opened the powerful SUV up taking full advantage of the deserted roads. Once back in town, the car continued to speed through the dark and windy streets, squealing around the corners. It wasn't long before they pulled up in front of Elsa's.

"You should be really glad that I'm getting you out of this shithole," Nick said as Bob got out of the car."

"Yeah, thanks, Nick, for everything," said Bob, trying not to sound sarcastic.

Bob didn't actually feel very much like thanking Nick, but he knew Nick expected it. Indeed, Nick's whole personality demanded it. But the more he learned about Nick the more disgusted he became. And it wasn't only with Nick, but also with himself. He had drunk way too much and felt sick to his stomach. He didn't like dealing with Nick, but what else could he do. Even though he wasn't quite sure why, he wasn't ready to go home yet. He didn't have much money. And unfortunately Nick was his only ticket to stay.

17

The Loganville Methodist Church threw the best spaghetti suppers in town, putting even the Sacred Heart Catholic Church with all its pasta-loving Italians to shame. The tradition started after the Second World War when a Methodist soldier from Loganville brought an Italian war bride home with him. Well, it wasn't long before she converted and put herself and her secret recipe for spaghetti sauce at the service of the Methodist Church. The supper, which had become a popular event on the town's fall social calendar, attracted hundreds of attendees from all around Logan County and raised thousands of dollars for the church. This year Connie, incapable of minding her own business and always ready to play the matchmaker, had brought Donna to introduce her to a nice man by the name of Earl Roberts whom Connie had met at a social at the church.

The church hall was all set up with long tables with red checkered tablecloths decorated with old Chianti bottles with candles, which was the way the good ladies of the Loganville First Methodist Church thought an authentic Italian eatery should look. Over at one end was a counter and pass-through into the kitchen out of which the same ladies were serving full plates of spaghetti and meatballs and bowls of Italian salad to a growing line of hungry people. Donna and Connie gave their tickets to a woman sitting at a table and joined the line.

"I feel silly about this," said Donna. "You think you're just gonna introduce me to this man and away we'll go happily like a couple of love-starved teenagers."

"Yeah, something like that," laughed Connie. "It works that way sometimes, you know. It's called sexual attraction."

"Please, spare me. I can't believe I'm doing this," complained Donna, rolling her eyes.

Soon they had worked their way up to the front of the line and were served. Taking their heaping plates to one of the tables, they sat down to eat.

"Where's the wine?" asked Donna.

"Some people in the church feel strongly that the consumption of alcoholic beverages is the root of all evil and others feel just as strongly that spaghetti must be served with red wine. Consequently, they've compromised and only serve wine every other year. Unfortunately for us, this is the off year."

"Oh, brother!" said Donna, taking a bite. A few seconds later, she smacked her lips and added, "Mmm! This is the best spaghetti!"

"What did I tell you?" said Connie, also starting to eat. "Obviously people don't come here in droves for the atmosphere." They weren't eating for long before Connie whispered, "Oh! Here he comes."

Donna looked over and could see a tall handsome man, with long dark curly hair, combed back, and sideburns, coming their way. He was impeccably dressed in a light blue seersucker suit, kind of like the one Bob sometime wore, but not wrinkled.

"Good evening, ladies," he said in a smooth deep courtly voice. "I'm pleased to meet you, Miss Blake. My name is Earl Roberts."

"I'm pleased to meet you too, Pastor Roberts," Donna said taking his extended hand. "Connie has told me many good things about you."

"And she's also spoken very highly about you," he replied. "Please just call me Earl. No need for the formality of Pastor."

"If you'll call me Donna," she said smiling, her resistance already starting to melt.

"Deal," he said, looking her directly in the eyes. Even though he was still holding her hand, she didn't pull away. He definitely had a certain magnetism that was difficult for her to resist.

The dinner served Connie's purpose. She had brought Donna and Earl together. All she had to do was stand back and let nature take its course. Before the evening was out, Earl had asked Donna out for the next Saturday night. Cupid's arrow was working its magic.

Bowling wasn't exactly what Donna had expected for a night out on the town. She hadn't been at Logan Lanes since high school. Thank goodness Earl had warned her to wear slacks, she thought. He was also very gentlemanly helping her to pick out shoes and a bowling ball. The balls seemed heavier than she remembered them, also more colorful. The one she picked out was purple with silver sparkles, like a giant-sized jawbreaker. Earl had brought his own more traditional black bowling ball. But the loose-fitting shirt with his name embroidered over his pocket that he wore was a nice touch that made him look like he was more than a casual bowler. Donna hoped she wasn't going to embarrass herself. Most of the lanes were busy, but lane six was vacant. They went over and Earl clipped the scorecard on the table.

"I hope you'll enjoy this," Earl said. "I've been bowling every Thursday night in the church league and have really gotten hooked."

"Well, it's been a long time for me. But it should be fun," Donna replied politely.

"I'm glad you feel that way. You go first."

"Okay."

With that Donna lifted the ball up behind her and took the customary three steps and let it go. The ball started down the center of the lane, but curved over to the side. By the time, it reached the end, it hit the four pin and only took three pins down.

Once the automatic pinsetter had cleared away the fallen pins and her ball had returned, she threw her second ball and knocked down five more pins, leaving only two standing.

"Pretty good," Earl said as he wrote down an eight in the box next to her name.

Picking the ball up in his left hand, he concentrated for a moment before starting his approach and powerfully sending the ball booming down the lane right into the pocket between the one and two pin. The pins crashed resoundingly into the backdrop for a strike.

"Wow!" said Donna. "I'm impressed. Do you always bowl this good?"

"No, but I try," he said.

The game went all right for Donna. At least there were no major disasters like dropping the ball on the backswing or falling down on the approach like she used to do in high school. She managed to eke out a 127. Respectable enough for a novice, she felt, but not in the same league as Earl who bowled a whopping 234. Maybe he was a bit of a showoff, but that was okay. She liked men that way, kinda flashy.

"Would you like to get something to drink before the next game?" he asked.

"Sure, I've worked up a real thirst," she said.

They went over to the bar, which was in a separate room at the front of the bowling alley. It was filled with bowlers celebrating their victories, forgetting their defeats, or whatever else bowlers do in a bar when they all get together.

"What do you want?" Earl asked.

"I'll have a Bud Lite," she said. "What are you gonna have?"

"I'll have a Coke," he said.

"Don't you like beer?" she asked.

"No, we don't drink alcoholic beverages in my church."

"Oh," she said awkwardly, sorry that she had asked.They exchanged small talk at the bar for a while before going back to bowl two more games. The second and third games went pretty much like the first, her score just over a hundred and his well over two hundred. Afterwards Earl drove Donna home. She invited him to come in for a while, but he politely declined saying he had to get home to work on his sermon for the next morning.

Donna's verdict after their first date was an unqualified maybe. She definitely wanted to get to know Earl better. What she had seen so far, she'd really liked. Even though he was a little shy, he was certainly attractive. He was handsome and athletically built. His piercing blue eyes seemed to look right into your soul. Yes, the physical attraction was definitely there. And she could feel it was reciprocal. She knew he'd call again for another date. A woman can always tell about such things.

The next Saturday morning Earl picked up Donna early in his twenty-year-old white Cadillac. They were going over to Turkey Run State Park in Indiana for a picnic. On their way out of town, they had to stop by Earl's house. His kids weren't awake when he had left and he needed to give them some last minute instructions before leaving. Or at least that was the pretext. He really wanted Donna to meet them.

Earl's house was a modest two-story brick structure on the other side of the tracks in the south end of town, not too far from his church. It was freshly painted and the yard was well maintained. He's obviously handy around the house, thought Donna, taking it all in carefully. Another plus she couldn't help ticking off in her mind. They entered through the side door into the kitchen. His two children were having a breakfast of bacon and eggs. The oldest, a pretty teenage girl with dark curly hair like her father, evidently knew how to cook. The younger one was a cute little freckled boy about nine or ten years old.

"I'd like you to meet my daughter Rebecca and my son Gordon," said Earl.

"Pleased to meet you, Ma'am," they both said very seriously, standing up to show respect the way children used to be taught to treat adults in the days before Dr. Spock.

"Glad to meet you, too," said Donna, smiling warmly to break the ice. The children responded by breaking into big smiles.

"Before we go," Earl said to the children, "I just wanted to remind you that Gordon has to read the book of Exodus for tomorrow's Bible study class. Rebecca, will you please help him out, if he needs any help?"

"Sure, Daddy, I will," she said, still standing.

"Okay," he said. "Now you both give me a kiss and I'll see you tonight." They dutifully came over and kissed their father, then went back over to the table to resume their breakfast. There was something military about the way he treated the children, but there was also true love and genuine affection. Donna was touched and impressed, yet somewhat taken aback.

"Your children are really nice and well behaved," said Donna, once they were back in the car and on their way.

"That's the way we brought them up—to be obedient and to respect their elders. We don't let them watch TV or go to movies or hang around the mall," he replied. "Rebecca has been a great help to me since her mother died. She cooks and cleans and looks after her younger brother."

Donna hesitated to tell him about Sarah. Was she too lenient with Sarah? Would Earl's brand of discipline work on Sarah? Maybe it was worth a try? She needed to do something different.

The one-hour drive to Turkey Run was enjoyable. It was a beautiful warm Indian summer day. The red and yellow fall foliage that draped Highway 41 was spectacular. When they got to the park, they left the car in the parking lot near the Nature Center and walked down to the Suspension Bridge. Crossing over, they followed the path at the bottom of the sandstone cliffs down along Sugar Creek where the big old sycamore trees grew."That large hollowed out area in the cliff over there is called the Ice Box," said Earl.

"It's neat the way that tree has grown up so straight and tall right next to the cliff, said Donna. "You come here often?"

"Not any more. But before my wife Betty died, we used to take the kids here all the time. There are not too many places left around where you can still see virgin forests like they have here. Mostly all you can see in these parts is corn," he laughed.

"What happened to Betty?" Donna asked as they walked, becoming serious.

"She died of breast cancer five years ago. She was only thirty-five. It was very hard on all of us, especially the kids," he said, his eyes becoming watery.

"I'm sorry," she said.

"Yes," he said. "She was a good obedient Christian wife and mother."

The words stunned Donna. Earl was clearly a man with quite different values from the others she had dated. What exactly did Earl mean? she thought. But she knew she couldn't ask him.

The trail turned up one of the ravines leading away from the river.

"We're gonna go up Bear Hollow. Don't worry about bears though. The last person to see one around here was probably Davy Crockett," said Earl.

"I'm more worried about climbing up the series of ladders I see going up the cliff," said Donna.

"You know these gorges are what gave the park its name," said Earl.

"How's that?"

"Back in pioneer times, wild turkeys would huddle in the ravines to keep warm. Hunters would herd them to the dead ends to shoot them. Turkey runs they called them."

"Oh, I always wondered where the name came from," said Donna.

"Are you ready for the ladders?" he asked.

"Sure," she said, taking a deep breath and starting to climb.

It was worth it to reach the top of the ridge. The trail wound through an old growth stand of black walnut trees before reaching a little creek.

"That's called the Punch Bowl," said Earl, pointing towards the creek. "It's a pothole made by a glacier."

The trail followed the creek through Rocky Hollow back to the Suspension Bridge and across to the parking lot where they had started.

"I guess it's time for lunch," said Donna. "I bet you're wondering what I've got in the cooler in the trunk."

"Sure am," he said hungrily.

"You'll have to wait and see," she teased.

Earl opened the trunk and carried the cooler over to one of the picnic tables. Donna opened it to reveal an old-fashioned, homemade lunch of fried chicken, potato salad and coleslaw. She gave Earl a paper plate, plastic spoon and a napkin and took the same for herself. Then she dished out heaping helpings on each of their plates. With full plates they sat down to eat.

"How did you decide to become a minister?" asked Donna, taking a dainty bite out of a crispy chicken leg.

"It was my calling ever since I was a boy. My Daddy was a minister. He was so proud the day I was ordained."

"Where did you go to become a minister?"

"The Cairo Bible College in Southern Illinois, the same place my Daddy went. That's where I met Betty. She was studying there, too."

"Oh," said Donna.

"I really wish you'd come to my church sometime. You could see what we do. I hope you might even find Jesus."

"Er...er...okay, if you really want me to, I guess I can come."

"I would be very pleased if you would. It would mean a lot to me. Also, I don't quite know how to say this, but could you please dress modestly like a good Christian woman? I'm not suggesting you wouldn't, of course, but unfortunately, some women do dress indecently and wear short skirts and low-cut tops. It's bad enough that they do this in public, but in a church it's scandalous."

"Don't worry," said Donna, thinking to herself that it's a good thing he hadn't seen some of her outfits, particularly the more sexy ones Bob liked the best.

"We've talked enough about me. What about you?" asked Earl.

Donna told him all about how she had grown up in Loganville, got married, had Sarah, and then divorced. She told him how she had lost her job as a hairdresser and was now working as a waitress. He listened intently. But somehow Donna forgot to mention Bob. Oh, well, a minor detail. No need to confuse the issue now, she rationalized.

After lunch, they took another hike. It was late afternoon before Earl dropped her off at her house. He held her hand as he walked her up to the door. When they got there, he reached his arms around her and started to give her a kiss. When she started to kiss him back, he recoiled.

"We mustn't go too fast," he said. "It wouldn't be right."

Donna pulled back in surprise. She had never seen a man fail to return a kiss. The problem had always been turning them off once they got started before they pulled your tonsils out with their tongue. Composing herself, she said, "Thank you, Earl, for a truly lovely day," as she went in the house. The attraction she felt to Earl was growing, but she wasn't sure about his religion and traditional ways. He was definitely not like the other men she had gone out with. He was going to take some getting used to.

The hall at Loganville High School was teeming with students. The bell had just rung and students were going to their lockers to get ready for their next classes or preparing to skip out early for lunch at one of the local hangouts. Sarah was standing in front of her locker looking for something. She was wearing low-riding jeans and a midriff-baring, pink short-sleeved shirt. Jessica who had the next locker came up next to her.

"Hi, Sarah. What's up?" Jessica said.

"Oh, hi, Jessie. I'm just trying to decide if I should go to study hall and finish the review of the *Great Gatsby* that I have to have ready for tomorrow's English class or if I should go over to Greenie's for a hamburger and fries."

"Duh! That's a real hard choice."

"Well, ordinarily it wouldn't be, but Mrs. Tilton called Mom and complained that I'd been skipping. Mom made me promise not to cut class."

"How's that motorcycle guy who got busted that you're hanging out with?"

"Oh, yeah, him…I dumped him. You know I found out it was him who sold the crack to poor dumb Tom. Can you imagine that, the slimeball. And all the time he'd been stringing me along telling me that the police had planted cocaine in his saddle bags. Dork that I was, I believed him."

"Did you tell your Mom?"

"No, not yet. She been too busy running around with some preacher guy. Somebody your mother introduced her to. She's been trying to get me to go to his church with her, but I'm not going. I don't want to encourage her. I'm hoping that Bob will come back. By default, he's become kind of a father figure for me. He talks to me, but he's not judgmental."

"C'mon, forget the *Great Gatsby* and let's go get a hamburger. I hear that cute new boy in our English class goes to Greenie's every day for lunch."

"Okay, okay, you've talked me into it. I can always do my homework later."

"You're starting to sound more like my old friend again."

18

Nick's plantation was right on the Northern Highway, but it seemed much farther off the beaten track. Perhaps that was because it was hidden in a jungle of sugar cane that could only be reached on a narrow track through a large locked metal gate. The plantation house, which was set in a big clearing, was built of whitewashed wood and had a wrap-around verandah. In front stood a flamboyant tree with its flaming red flowers. Surrounding the house were thick bougainvilleas with their vibrant purple flowers in full bloom. Several majestic guanacaste trees shaded the yard. Four large barn-like outbuildings were strategically placed in the corners. Men were working nearby and three trucks were parked on the gravel in front of the largest of the outbuildings. Behind the house was a kidney shaped swimming pool, which was barely visible behind a hedge of oleander.

As the SUV approached the house, two large German shepherds materialized from out of nowhere with fangs bared and began barking loudly.

"Don't worry," said Jules, getting out of the car. "I'll take care of them. Stop that," he yelled with the authority of a master. The dogs, who were evidently very well trained, not like Toto, immediately assumed a submissive posture with their ears back and tails down. "Go lay down," he said. And the dogs slumped back under the porch to sleep.

"I'm glad you're here," said Bob. "Those goddamn dogs looked pretty mean."

"We've trained them to be mean. That's what keeps people out. They're good watchdogs."

Jules then went around to the back of the SUV and got Bob's suitcase out.

"Follow me, and I'll show you where you'll be staying," he said.

Bob followed Jules into the very large house, which was new and modern on the inside, but built in the style of a Caribbean great house on the outside. Down a series of long halls they went to a room in the back. In contrast with the rest of the house, which was very well appointed, with antiques and genuine art on the walls, the room was Spartan. Jules put the suitcase on a stand in the corner.

"The office is down the hall," Jules said. "Mr. Devlin told me to tell you that he'll be out tonight to show you what he wants you to do. He said that, in the meantime, you can just chill out."

"Thanks," said Bob.

After Jules left, Bob unpacked his suitcase and hung his clothes in the closet. He then went out on the porch and walked around the house taking stock of his new surroundings. The sweet smell of the oleander shrubs permeated the air. Bob could see the men going in and out of the large building on the southeast corner of the clearing. What the devil were they doing? he wondered. When he reach the back of the house, he found the swimming pool. There he saw Nick's girlfriend, Luna, sitting in a lounge chair in a low-cut, flowered sundress, reading a well-thumbed copy of *Cosmopolitan.*

Laying down the magazine on the glass-topped table next to her, she smiled flirtatiously and said, "Hi, Bob, Nick told me you'd be coming out. He's told me a lot about you, you know."

"Oh, he has, has he? Well, he didn't tell me you'd be here," said Bob, looking a little bit uneasy. He knew that Luna was Nick's girl and that prudence dictated that he stifle any physical attraction he might feel for Luna. And then, if more were needed to keep him in line, there was the thought of Donna waiting loyally for him back home.

"I've been buried out here for a while. Nick seems to want to keep me out of town for some reason."

"Is that so bad? There are a cook and a housekeeper out here to take care of everything we need. Aren't there?" asked Bob.

"Yeah, you're right. The food and accommodations are pretty good, but it gets a bit boring after a while. That's why I'm sure glad you'll be out here to keep me company," she said.

"I don't know how good company I'll be. Nick's got a lot of pretty tedious work he wants me to do while I'm here."

"Well, Nick said you'd have some time," she pouted.

"Okay, if that's what he said, I'm sure we'll have some time to get to know one another better."

"Good. Then it's settled," she said, smiling. "Why don't you sit down and we can talk."

"All right," said Bob, plopping himself down in the lounge chair next to her.

Later that night when Bob and Luna were just finishing dinner, Nick arrived from town and stormed into the dining room with a scowl on his face.

"You two look like you're getting pretty chummy," he said.

"What else can we do?" said Luna. "We're stuck out here in the goddamn middle of nowhere with nobody but each other for company."

"All you ever do anymore, Luna, is complain," shouted Nick. "I'm getting sick and tired of it. I've got a good mind to throw you back into the gutter I found you in. Now get the hell out of here. We've got some man business to do."

Luna sulked out of the room without protesting, but looking very resentful.

"Why do you treat her like that?" Bob asked. "She seems like a nice enough girl."

"I can treat her any way I like," Nick said peevishly. "If it weren't for me, she'd still be working in the Paradise Club."

"Sorry, Nick. I didn't mean to interfere."

"Good, as long as you can remember that, we'll get along much better."

After this rocky start for their new business arrangement, Nick escorted Bob into the office in the back of the house. The door was locked and the room had no windows. Nick opened it and gave Bob a key. Inside were two white metal filing cabinets, an old rolltop desk with a ledger book on top, and several boxes direct from the manufacturer containing a computer, a monitor, and a printer.

"Your job is to take that ledger and set up a bookkeeping system on the computer with exactly the same accounts. After you do that, I want you to show our bookkeeper Frederico how to use it. He comes out from town every week to do our books."

"That shouldn't be too difficult," said Bob.

"Good," said Nick. "How long will it take?"

"Depends, but shouldn't be longer than a couple of weeks."

"Okay, but remember, anything you learn about my business, it stays here on the plantation."

"Sure, of course, Nick, anything you say," said Bob.

"I do say so. And I really mean it," said Nick. "Trust me."

"Okay, I promise. I was wondering if before I start work, you'd mind if I took a ride over to Altun Ha to see the ruins," said Bob. "I've already seen a couple of Mayan sites and have been doing a little reading about the Maya. I don't want to miss seeing Altun Ha after all I've heard about it, particularly since it's so close. Maybe Luna could come along. She's told me she's been there before and offered to give me a little tour."

"Okay," said Nick. "I'll get one of the men to drive you over tomorrow morning. But be back before noon. Remember, you're here to work and not to sightsee."

The next morning Bob and Luna left the compound in the back of an SUV driven by a very taciturn and sullen-looking Mestizo named Jorge. They drove up towards Orange Walk on the Northern Highway and then turned south on the Old Northern Highway, which ran to the coast. It was about a forty-five minute drive to Altun Ha. When they got there, Jorge stayed in the car in the parking lot with the motor running and had a smoke. Bob and Luna got out to see the site.

Walking towards it, they passed by a fruit tree filled with a flock of blue buntings. As they got closer, Bob and Luna followed the narrow path through the bush between two of the structures and came out in a plaza surrounded by five pyramids.

"The largest one over there is the Temple of the Green Tomb," said Luna, pointing towards the far side of the plaza. "Quite a few artifacts were found inside it, including jewelry and part of an ancient Mayan book. You want to climb it?"

"No, I'm saving myself for the Temple of the Masonry Altars. That's what I really came to see," said Bob.

Taking him by the hand, she led him on a path between two pyramids at the south end of the plaza and they emerged into the second plaza. On their left, at the far end of the plaza, stood the Temple of the Masonry Altars, which was also known as the Temple of the Sun God. It was much more intact than the other pyramids that Bob had seen, in part because of the extensive restoration work that had been done. The bottom tier of the limestone structure had steps running its whole length. On top was a unique round altar. Bob and Luna walked over and climbed the steps sixty feet to the top.

"After Lamanai and Xunantunich, this is a bit of a letdown," said Bob after they reached the top. "These pyramids are nowhere near as spectacular and neither is the view."

"No," said Luna. "But remember, this is the pyramid where they found the jade head of Kinich Ahau, the Mayan Sun God. It was buried in a tomb next to the body of a Mayan priest."

"Yes," said Bob. "I knew that. In fact, that's why I came. I saw the jade head in Belize City and was curious to see where it actually came from."

For the next few days, Bob fell into the routine of getting up early in the morning and going down to the kitchen. There Alicia, the plump cook who always wore a flowered tent-like shift, would have a pot of coffee and basket of rolls ready for him as he had requested. With his breakfast in hand, he would retreat to the locked room for a morning's work. While Nick's ledger had a lot of strike-outs and erasures, it was legible enough for him to get the information he required to create the computerized accounts. This was not a very challenging job for a CPA from Illinois, especially for one who had just dealt with the disorderly books of the crippled children's project.

The afternoons he spent lolling around the pool with Luna. He was really getting to like her, but he still worried about getting too close out of fear of Nick.

At night, sometimes he would hear activity in the yard as trucks came and went and men yelled back and forth. One night he heard something that sounded like a plane flying low over the house. What is going on around here? he wondered.

The next day Bob decided to take a walk around the plantation to learn a bit more about his surroundings. When he got out behind the barn, he found a well-trodden path leading into the bush. When he had gone about fifty feet, he ran into three squat men carrying machetes coming the other way.

"¿Donde va?" challenged one of the men wearing a big straw hat.

Bob kept walking toward the men as he did not understand what the man had said.

"No pasa," the man said motioning menacingly with the machete to go back.

Bob was beginning to get the point when the two other men each grabbed an arm and forcefully turned him around and pushed him back up the path.

That afternoon by the pool, he told Luna what he had heard at night and what had happened in the morning. "What's going on around here?" he asked.

"You really don't know, do you?" she asked.

"No, I don't," he replied.

"It's the business."

"What business?" he asked with astonishment. "Isn't this a sugar plantation?"

"Sure, it's a sugar plantation " she said. "That's why there's sugar cane growing all around."

"What does sugar cane have to do with trucks going back and forth at night and planes flying overhead?" he asked.

"Sugar prices being what they are, people have to, er...shall we say, supplement their income with other activities."

"Whaddaya mean?" he asked.

"Well, they grow a few other things."

"Like what?" he asked.

"Like bush," she said.

"You mean marijuana!"

"Yeah, and since they're sending that up to the States, they figure they might as well throw in a little cocaine they get from Colombia, which is a lot more valuable."

"How do they get the drugs into the United States?" asked Bob.

"You heard the plane, didn't you? They have a Cessna 192 they keep out in the old barn near the Northern Highway. There are other planes that come in occasionally as well to make pick-ups or drop-offs."

"How do they take the planes off and land them?" he asked.

"The Northern Highway. It's flat and straight. It makes a perfect runway after you cut down all the poles that the meddling government keeps putting up next to the road to try to stop planes from landing."

"What about the cars on the road?"

"Oh, that's no problem. They just stop the traffic and give people a few dollars to keep their mouths shut. Nobody is going to argue with Nick's gunmen. Those who have in the past have usually ended up in a shallow grave decorated with Kohune palm fronds."

"Oh, my God," said Bob, as the light finally went on in his head.

"Yeah," said Luna. "You poor boy. You're really in a bit over your head, aren't you?"

"You can say that again!" asserted Bob.

"What are you gonna do?" asked Luna, patting him sympathetically on the back.

"I don't know," he said, holding his head in his hands and staring blankly in the water. What have I gotten myself into this time? he thought. Am I ever gonna get out of here?

Like the good and dutiful accountant he was, Bob continued his daily routine working on the computerization of the books. But now he started to notice things. For instance, he could see that the books only covered the revenues from the sugar plantation, the cattle ranch, the citrus grove, and the logging operation. Nothing was on the books, of course, for selling marijuana or trafficking cocaine. He wondered how much Nick made from these illegal activities. It must have been a lot to cover the purchases of all the properties he owned, which Bob could see were financed by loans from offshore companies. Must be the old boomerang trip I'd read about in one of the journals on forensic accounting, Bob thought. I'll bet he makes good use of the casino, too. Nick sure knows how to launder money!

A few days later, Bob and Luna were sitting by the pool drinking daiquiris. "Where are you from?" he asked.

"I grew up down in Nicaragua in a town called Bluefields. It's inhabited by English-speaking people like in Belize. After I finished high school, I came up here to look for a job that paid better than back home. I didn't get much work but I sure got mixed up with some people who, let's just say, weren't very nice. They lent me some money to tide me over. Then when I couldn't pay them back, they forced me to work at the Paradise Club. That's where Nick found me. He came a few times as a client. I liked him because he was nice to me and seemed like a pretty good guy. I was really flattered when he asked me to go away with him. I thought that maybe we had something going. But it was all wishful thinking. It wasn't long before he started to treat me like his personal whore, which is what I guess he wanted me for."

"Why don't you run away?"

"I don't have any money and besides he'd probably catch me. Then I'd be even worse off, if not dead," she replied.

In the tough Yarborough section of Belize City, or "Yabra" as it is called locally, Nick, accompanied by Jules and two other men all carrying micro Uzi submachine guns, strolled into one of the "Negro houses," which are made up of long rows of rooms with a common roof. Inside he confronted a young gang chief who was backed up by five of his men, all decked out in red bandannas—their gang colors.

"Hey, maan," the cocky young gang chief said.

"Don't 'hey, maan' me, Norman. What happened to the money for the last load of bush we sent you," asked Nick.

"Problems, maan. Ya know how 'tis."

"Yeah, I know how it is, but I don't care about your problems," retorted Nick.

"Don' be that way, maan. We been thinkin', maybe we could get a better deal from the Hondurans. Dey now be moving some bush into B-Town."

At this, Nick's eyes flashed. Quickly reaching under his coat, he pulled out a .45-caliber pistol and in an explosive rage struck Norman across the face. Blood poured out of Norman's nose as he toppled to the ground. The gang stood submissively by while Nick kicked Norman a couple of times in the stomach as he writhed on the ground with blood now coming out of his mouth as well. The normally aggressive gang members were paralyzed by their fear of Nick and his men. Like a troop of hyenas, they knew enough to stand well back when a lion was at work.

Pointing his gun at the others, Nick asked, "Do any of you share Norman's desire to find a new business partner?"

"No, maan, no, maan," they all said, shaking their heads vigorously.

"Fine," said Nick. "I think I can work with you guys as long as you remember our little lesson today about business etiquette. Which one of you wants to be in charge now?"

One of the boys looked around at the others and seeing no challengers, stepped forward.

"I guess me, sir," he said.

"And who are you?" asked Nick.

"I Danny, sir," said the boy.

"Okay, Danny-boy, if that's your name," said Nick. "You'll have to do provided you can get me full payment by next week. And I'm warning you the next time there's any funny business, I'm not gonna be as understanding."

"You de boss, sir," said the new leader. "We di pay you. We no tief you money."

19

It was a moonlit night and Bob and Luna were sitting alone at the dining room table talking after dinner. Celine Dion singing "My Heart Will Go On" came on the radio. The music, which started softly, was powerful and romantic.

"Would you like to dance?" asked Luna, moved by the music and moonlight.

"I'm not much of a dancer, but if you'd like, how can I refuse," Bob replied.

The two got up. Bob took Luna's hand and put his other hand around her waist. She put her arm around his shoulder and touched his neck like Donna did. Their bodies swayed in rhythm to the slow beat of the music. Bob could feel Luna's pelvis and breasts rubbing against his body. She put her head on his shoulder. It made him feel very manly to hold her smaller, more vulnerable, female body so close. What a beautiful woman she was! As beautiful as any he had ever met. He didn't want the dance ever to stop, but the song ended. Still holding her in his arms, he hesitated to release her.

The magic of this intimate moment was spoiled by a commercial for Belikan Beer, which came blaring out from the radio. Bob let Luna go. Maybe that was for the best. He was letting himself get too hot and bothered. Better sit down and cool off before things get out of control, thought Bob. If I know what's good for me, I've got to get a hold of myself. Gotta remember she's Nick's girl, he reminded himself.

They sat back down at the table and poured themselves a drink. A long silence passed while Luna sized him up. She was trying to decide how much she liked him and whether she could trust him. He seemed to be a square guy, pretty transparent, not like Nick. Impulsively deciding to go with her woman's instincts, Luna got up and motioned with her hand for Bob to come. Although he was surprised by her action, he allowed her to take his hand and lead him down the corridor to a door that went down into the basement. At the bottom of the steps was another door. Pulling a key out of her décolletage, Luna opened it.

"Why so mysterious?" Bob asked. "What's in there?"

"Just look," she said, flipping the light switch.

To Bob's amazement, he saw shelves covered with a variety of Mayan artifacts just like in a museum. There was pottery, and gold and jade jewelry. His eyes were quickly drawn to a large jade head that sat alone on the top shelf.

"Is that for real?" he asked with surprise.

"Sure is," she said.

"Wow! It looks a lot like the statue of the Sun God, Kinich Ahau, that I saw at the Bliss Institute," said Bob, going over to pick it up and take a closer look. As he turned it in his hand, he could see that while it was the same color and size, the carved face looked different. "But it's not the same. Hey! What is it?"

"Nick told me it's the head of Ixchel, the moon goddess. She's the wife of the Sun God. To the Mayans, she represents the female force in the universe."

"Where did he get it?"

"It was found in a dig at a ruins on this very plantation back near the Revenge Lagoon. That's where all these artifacts come from. They've been excavating there at night for almost a year. As soon as they can finalize the sales arrangements with a rich collector in Columbia, they're gonna ship them out of here by plane."

"Well, I'll be damned!" he said. "Do you know how much that jade head is worth?"

"No, but I suspect a lot. Enough probably to set me up for life. And enough for you, too," she said, looking pleadingly in Bob's eyes. "Willya help me steal it?"

"Whoa! Whoa! Hold your horses. Is that why you softened me up with that dance and brought me down here? So that you could try to sweet talk me into this? Surely you know we'd never be able to pull it off without Nick catching us?"

"Just keep an open mind and listen to my plan before you decide. After we slip the jade head out of this room, all we have to do to escape is to take one of the plantation trucks and go up to Orange Walk Town and catch the first plane out for Mexico. By the time Nick comes back to check, we can be long gone with the jade head."

"I don't know. What if he catches us? He'd crucify us. Or worse."

"He's not gonna catch us. Don't worry about that. Think instead about all the money we're gonna have to spend."

"No! No! I just can't do it," said Bob, who was not a person who was used to taking such big risks.

The next day Bob sat on the deck alone drinking rum and pondering his plight. What a mess I've gotten myself into this time! he thought. Here I am trapped on a plantation in the middle of the jungle. Will Nick really let me go when I finish my work? Can I escape? And what about the jade head? Bob couldn't get it out of his mind. His thoughts were brought abruptly back to reality by the sound of Nick pulling up in his SUV. As Bob looked on with mixed feelings of fear and guilt, Nick got out and joined him on the deck. Casually pouring himself a tumbler of rum from the bottle on the table and lighting up a Cuban cigar, Nick sat down comfortably in the chair next to Bob and exhaled a big cloud of smoke.

"You look like you've just seen a ghost?" Nick said. "Aren't you glad to see me?"

"Oh, no, no, Nick. It's nothing. I'm just feeling a little sick. Perhaps it was something I ate," he replied a little nervously, fearing that Nick could read his mind by the look on his face.

"How's the work coming?" Nick asked, puffing out a thick ring of smoke.

"It should be done next week," said Bob. "Then I'll be going back to Belize City."

"Not so fast," said Nick. "I'd like you to stay around for a few more weeks. There are a few more things I'd like you to tidy up."

"Well, er...I guess I can if you really want, Nick," Bob stammered, "but er...I'm really gonna have to be going pretty soon."

"I'll tell you when you're done and can go," Nick said peremptorily.

That night after he retired to his room, Bob could hear noises coming through the wall from Luna's room.

"You ungrateful bitch!" shouted Nick.

"No! Nick, no! Ow! Ow!"

Visions of his drunk father beating his mother flashed through Bob's mind. Why did I ever got involved with Nick? he asked himself. What could I have ever been thinking? Some Hemingwayesque adventure I got myself into. Later that night, as he lay sleepless on his bed, he heard Nick's SUV leaving noisily. Thank God he's going! Bob thought.

When Bob saw Luna the next day in the hall in the morning, her face was all swollen up.

"Did he hit you?" he asked, sympathetically.

She nodded affirmatively, sobbing.

"I'm sorry," he said putting his arm around her to comfort her as she cried softly on his shoulder.

That bastard, thought Bob.

A few nights later Bob and Luna were again sitting in the dining room after dinner drinking rum and commiserating.

"Do you think Nick will ever let us go?" asked Bob.

"He may let me go when he gets tired of me. But he'll probably kill you when you're done with your work. You know just too much for your own good now," she replied matter-of-factly.

"Do you really think so?" asked Bob, with an alarmed look on his face.

"Yes, I do," she answered

"You're not very encouraging," Bob said, plaintively.

"I'm just telling you the truth. You know full well your only chance is to escape with me. And you also should know that I'm not going anywhere without the jade head. It's our future."

Bob sat quietly for a few minutes thinking. Then he said "The way I see it, I'm kinda caught between a rock and a hard place. If I stay here, Nick will get me for sure. If I go with you, he'll probably catch us both. But I guess you're right. It's my only chance. I've got no other choice but to do it."

"All right, now you're talking my language. Let's get our bags ready and then go downstairs to pick up the jade head," she said.

"Okay," he said weakly, even though he had a funny feeling in the pit of his stomach that warned him he was probably making a big mistake.

Bob went to his room and threw all his clothes in his bag. He stuffed his passport and wallet in his back pockets. I must be crazy, he thought, starting to hyperventilate. Stay calm, breathe slowly, remember, grace under pressure, he told himself. Five minutes later, when he was finished packing and had calmed down, he met Luna in the hall. Leaving their bags, they went down into the basement to the room where the jade head was stored.

"Oh, no!" said Luna. "We'll never be able to get it now."

"What's wrong?" asked Bob.

"Nick must have suspected something was up. He had a padlock put on the door. It's a combination lock and I don't know the combination."

"Do you know where he keeps the combination?" asked Bob.

"Maybe," said Luna. "He keeps some papers in his desk. I'll run up and check."

In what seemed like an hour to Bob, who was on the verge of an anxiety attack, but was really only five minutes, Luna returned with a paper in her hand.

"What's this?" asked Bob, looking at the scrap of paper Luna was holding in her hand.

On it, he could see the symbols:

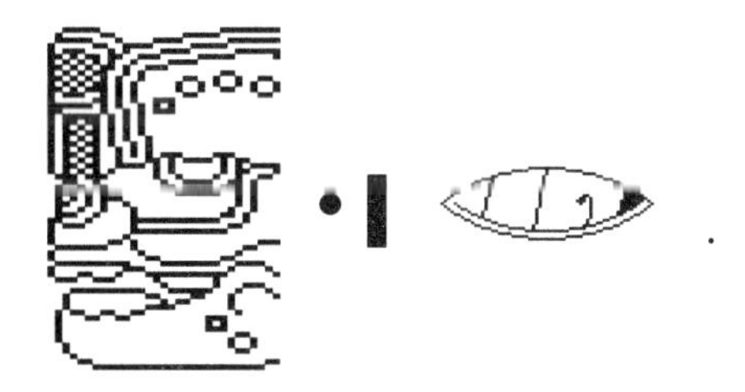

They both stood there, scratching their heads over the strange hieroglyphics. Then all of a sudden a light went off in Bob's head. "Hey! I know those symbols from Dr. Butterfield's book," said Bob. "The first is the glyph of Lahun, the death lord, which symbolizes the number ten. The dot and the bar represent six and the shell zero. Let me try the padlock," he said, turning the dial three times right past zero to ten, twice left past zero to six, and finally right to zero. The padlock clicked open. "We did it! We did it!" he blurted out triumphantly.

"Shh!" said Luna. "The men are going to hear us and come running."

"Oh, I'm sorry," said Bob sheepishly. "Let's go in and get it and get the hell out of here."

Rushing over and quickly scooping the jade head off the shelf, Bob wrapped it tightly in a T-shirt and put it under his arm like a football. Then he stopped and, becoming very serious, said to Luna, "Wait. I don't know if we should continue. The symbol of the death lord freaks me out. I'm afraid it may be trying to tell us something."

"Don't be silly. It's too late to turn back now," said Luna. "We've got to keep going."

"I guess you're right," said Bob without much enthusiasm.

Retracing their steps up the stairs and stopping to pick up their bags in the hall, Bob and Luna stealthily went out on the verandah. The moon shone brightly in the sky illuminating the landscape.

"I've got the key to that truck," she said, pointing towards a truck parked next to one of the outbuildings.

Bob and Luna ran over to the truck, threw their bags in the back, and climbed in the cab. The jade head was still held tightly under Bob's arm. Luna was in the driver's seat. When she turned the key, the truck turned over but didn't start. A light went on in the building and the dogs started barking. She tried again. This time the engine sputtered a few times.

"Hurry up!" Bob urged her frantically.

"I'm trying," she said. "It just doesn't seem to want to start."

"¿Que pasa?" a voice yelled..

"Alguien esta en el camion," replied the other voice.

Luna tried the key again. The truck started. She gunned it and the tires began to spin wildly, throwing up a stream of gravel. The truck stood still for a moment and then lurched toward the gate. The two men came running. Shots rang out. A bullet broke the back windshield and hit Luna. The truck careened out of control. It only came to a stop when it crashed into a tree near the gate. Bob's head smashed into the dashboard. It hurt and stunned him, but it wasn't hard enough to knock him out. He looked over at Luna slumped over the steering wheel. Even in the dim moonlight he could see her beautiful braided black hair stained red with blood.

"Oh, my God," he said, feeling sick to his stomach. But this was not the time for horror or grief. The sound of approaching footsteps and voices told him he'd better do something and fast or both he and Luna were finished. Bob's survival instincts kicked into action. He reached over Luna and awkwardly grabbed the steering wheel. Shifting into reverse, he backed rapidly away from the tree almost running over the approaching men, who jumped out of the way in the nick of time. Then putting the gearshift back into drive and pushing on the gas, he maneuvered the truck across the yard and smashed through the gate. A couple of more shots rang out. The truck started to swerve. The right back tire had been hit. But this wasn't enough to stop Bob. He continued to drive the truck out to the main highway. Riding bumpily on the rim, he managed to make it about a mile up the Northern Highway before he felt safe enough to pull over and to try and see what he could do for Luna.

She was still breathing, and moaning. Bob laid her on the seat and examined her. Turning her on her side, he could see the a gaping hole in the back of her head. "Oh, my God!" Bob exclaimed. "Luna, Luna," he cried, but there was no reply. He wrapped his arms around her and held her, not knowing what else he could do. It wasn't long before her breath stopped. Bob knew that she had left this world. "Oh, Luna," he said. "I should've never let you do this. It's all my fault." Continuing to hold her, he sobbed to himself until his grief was interrupted by lights in the truck mirror. Oh, no! he thought. They're coming. What am I gonna do? He knew that he couldn't outrun them in a truck with only three tires. The only thing left for him to do was to run and hide in the bush.

Laying Luna's body on the seat, Bob kissed her softly good-bye. "I'm sorry to have to leave you like this," he said, "but there's nothing more I can do for you." Picking up the package containing the jade head on the floor where it had fallen, Bob opened the truck door and slipped out onto the ground like one of the ninjas he'd seen in a Japanese martial arts movie. A cane field was only twenty feet away. Scrambling like a frightened three-legged mouse, he made for the field. When he reached it, he looked back and could see another truck filled with men and dogs pulling up behind his truck.

Staggering to his feet, Bob took off running for his life into the high cane. He could hear the dogs barking behind him as he ran. The thick cane tore his pants and shirt as he ran. Coming across a path visible in the moonlight, he headed back into the bush towards the lagoon. The barking became fainter. Thank God the dogs weren't bloodhounds, he thought. He stopped to wipe the sweat off his forehead with his sleeve. He could see that there was blood on it. He must have cut his head when it hit the dashboard. Mosquitoes were swarming all around, feasting on his exposed skin. Bob started running again deeper into the bush. Branches and thorns tore his clothes and flesh as he ran. His heart was racing faster and faster and his breathing became heavier and heavier. Coming to a small river, he could see the glowing form of the moon mirrored in the water. Jumping in, he started to wade across. The water was warm like a bath. It got deeper and deeper. Finally he had to swim, which was very difficult for him to do wearing shoes and carrying the jade head. But it wasn't very far, and, fueled by adrenaline, he was somehow able to make it to the other side. Gasping and coughing up water, he scrambled up the bank and collapsed on the ground. A frightening roar disturbed the quiet of the night and got him on his feet and moving again. It must be a jaguar, thought Bob. And it sounded close. Too close for comfort. Had he eluded his pursuers only to fall prey to a giant spotted cat? Bob took off running again. But he didn't get very far before he tripped over a log and hit his head. There he lay alongside a bush road in a state of semi-consciousness with the jade head still clutched tightly under his arm. Only the moon in the sky watched over him.

Two men picked Bob up off the ground. They were dressed in loincloths decorated with feathers and Mayan designs and wore double-thonged leather sandals bound to their ankles with ropes. Their bodies were painted black and red and necklaces adorned their chests. They dragged Bob through the bush into a clearing. A pyramid lit with torches stood at the end of the plaza. It looked like the Temple of the Masonry Altars. The warriors hauled Bob over to the stairs leading up to the ceremonial altar and roughly stripped off his clothes. He tried to resist as they forced him up the steps one by one, but it was useless. They were too strong. At the top were two more warriors in full regalia. They grabbed Bob and painted his body blue. Then the four warriors acting together threw Bob on his back on a rounded sacrificial stone and held him down. A priest came out wearing a jaguar skin and a headdress made out of a jaguar's head. He had the jade head in one hand and a flint knife in another.

"You stole the head of our Moon Goddess, Ixchel, and you must pay with your blood," said the priest.

"No, please," pleaded Bob. Before his eyes the face of priest was transformed into the laughing face of Nick.

The priest took the flint knife and made an incision on the left side of his chest. Bob felt a sharp pain below his nipple. Right before his eyes, the priest reached in and tore out his beating heart and anointed the jade head with his blood. Then Bob felt his head spinning and spinning as his naked body was pushed off the sacrificial stone and rolled down the steps of the temple. Nick's hysterical laugh resonated in his ears as he tumbled. He came to rest at the bottom next to a naked, skinned female body. He looked at the face. To his horror, it was Luna.

"No! God, no!" he raved. His bug-bitten and scratched body was ravaged by a fever and drenched in sweat.

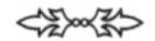

20

Early the next morning a black buggy drawn by a dark brown horse with a white nose came clippity-clopping along the bush track. The sight of a body laying at the side of the road spooked the horse and it started to rear up. The driver, a clean-shaven, sandy-haired man dressed in denim overalls and wearing a white straw hat, pulled on the reins and uttered reassuringly in a firm voice, "Whoa! Gerda, whoa!" When the horse had finally calmed down, the driver climbed down from the seat and walked over to examine the body. As the driver got closer, he could see that it was a man and he was alive.

"Mister, Mister, are you all right?" he asked putting his face down close to the man's and putting his hands on the man's forehead, which he could feel was burning up.

"Ohhh!" moaned the man, still trapped in his horrible nightmare.

"I can't leave you out here," the driver said. "Reckon I'd better take you home."

With his muscular arms hardened by a lifetime of outdoor work, the driver easily picked the injured man up and laid him down in the back of the buggy. Turning around, he headed the horse back up the track the same way he had come. It was only a few miles and they arrived at a large wooden house with a barn attached. The house was painted white with a corrugated tin roof. It sat on the banks of a river. Three young blond-headed children came running out to greet the buggy. The two boys were wearing overalls and a straw hat like the driver. The girl was wearing a long cotton print dress and an organdy cap tied tightly under her chin.

"Vater, Vater, why are you back so soon?" they asked in unison, speaking Low German, an old dialect long forgotten, even in Germany.

"I found an injured man along the side of the road and I've brought him home to take care of him. Tell your mother to get the guest bedroom ready," the driver replied in the same archaic German tongue.

Allowing time for this message to be relayed and acted upon, the driver waited. Then he picked up the man and took him through the front door and into one of the bedrooms in the back of the house. There he laid him on the bed. With the help of his wife, he took off the man's clothes, washed the blood and dirt off him, and picked off a few ticks that had burrowed into his body. Then they treated his many bug-bites and lacerations with some kind of homemade balm. All the while, the man was mumbling incoherently, something about a jade head, the moon, and death. Finally they put the man in a nightshirt and covered him up with a sheet. Leaving the room quietly, they left him to rest. If he didn't show signs of improvement soon, they would get a doctor.

That night Bob awoke startled, all covered in sweat in a room lit by a kerosene lamp. It was sparsely furnished, containing only a chest of drawers, a bedside table and a single wooden chair, all made of mahogany, as was the bed frame. No pictures were on the wall. Had everything that happened been a giant nightmare? Bob asked himself. Was Luna still alive?

"Hello, hello," Bob shouted. "Is anybody here?"

The man and woman ran into the room. "Oh! You seem to be getting better. Maybe you won't need a doctor after all," the man said.

"No! No! Don't call a doctor," said Bob, afraid that this would just call attention to his whereabouts. "I'll be fine. I just need a little rest."

"Don't worry," the man said. "We don't like doctors any more than you."

"Who are you?" Bob asked.

"I'm Johann Friesen and this is my wife Mia."

"Where am I?"

"You're at our home in Shipyard."

"Where's that?"

"It's on the west bank of the New River, upstream from Orange Walk."

"Did I have a bundle with me?" Bob asked anxiously.

"Yes, a very heavy one," Johann answered. "I put it in the chest drawer for you."

"Thank you," said Bob, breathing a sigh of relief. But his feeling of relief was quickly crowded out of his consciousness by the full horror of what had happened. Everything was not a dream, he realized. Luna really is dead. I shouldn't have let her do it. It was way too dangerous. I'm not superstitious, but maybe I should have heeded the warning of the glyph of Lahun. It's strange that Luna was killed and not me. Ixchel is supposed to represent the feminine life force. Yet the same moon that guided me to safety provided the light to shoot Luna.

"Are you all right?" asked Johann.

"Yes," said Bob, coming back out of his tormented inner world to focus on Johann's words. Composing himself, he said, "I've asked you a lot of questions. I suppose you have a few for me."

"No," said Johann. "I'm sure if there is anything we need to know the Lord will reveal it to us in the fullness of time. It was his will that we find you lying by the road and bring you here."

"Well, I don't know about that, but I'm certainly grateful. Thank you. By the way, my name is Bob Wayne and I'm from the United States. I need to call home. Can I use your phone? I can call collect."

"I'm sorry, but we have no telephone."

"That's too bad. There's someone I really need to talk to. I guess I'll have to go home to do it."

"I'm afraid you're not in any condition to go anywhere right now. But we'd be glad to have you stay with us for a few days until you recover," said Johann.

"I'm a little worried about some people finding me. Will I be safe here?" asked Bob.

"Don't worry," said Johann. "We live in a very private and closed community and outsiders don't come around very often."

"Good, I'm very grateful to accept your kind offer to let me stay here until I recover."

The next morning when he woke up, Bob was famished, even though his spirit was still weighed down by Luna's murder. Before he had to ask for food, Mia brought in a tray containing a hearty breakfast of fresh eggs, sausage, toast and coffee. She did not stay while he ate, but shyly put the tray on the bedside table, carefully avoiding eye contact. Bob picked up the tray and ate heartily. The food tasted so good and it had been such a long time since he had eaten.

After eating, he dozed off again into another bout of troubled sleep. He was awakened by giggling. It was the three children peeking through the door at him. They were evidently amused at the sight of a stranger in their house. Mia came to the door holding a baby and shooed them away.

"Let Mr. Wayne sleep, children," she said. "They'll be plenty of time to see him when he is awake. Rachel, you can come and help me in the kitchen; we have a lot of oranges that have to be made into marmalade. And Peter and Aron, you have your chores to do. The eggs need to be gathered and the animals fed."

Turning to Bob, she said, "Don't mind the children, Mr. Wayne, they've never seen an English person in their house."

"English? Is that what you call us—'English'?" Bob asked."Yes," she said. "You're not one of us."

Later that day, Johann saw a truck drive by the house. He told Bob that there were two strange men in it, looking all around. Uh-oh, it must be Nick's men, thought Bob.

Bob dozed and ate for three days as he gradually regained his strength. Mia regularly brought him his meals, but never talked much. Johann would come by and visit now and then when he had some free time from his work. As Bob got stronger and was able to move about dressed in clothes he had borrowed from Johann, he became more curious about the Friesen's lifestyle. The house had no electricity or telephone. No photographs of family members or ancestors were displayed. A leather-bound copy of Luther's German language Bible sat prominently on the sideboard in the living room. The kitchen had a big black wood stove and chimney. The barn attached to the house had stables and stalls for cattle. Chickens scratched for food in the yard and pigs rooted in the pen out back. A large fenced-in garden was right next to the house. The family was very self-sufficient at a subsistence level. But everybody, including the children, seemed to be working constantly. It sure didn't look like an easy life to someone like Bob accustomed to the joys of modern living.

Standing next to the barn, Bob asked Johann. "How did you end up living here?"

"We're Old Colony Mennonites," said Johann. "We've had to move around a lot to be free to practice our religion. We moved from Germany to Chortitza in South Russia in the eighteenth century. Then in the late nineteenth century the Czar reneged on his promise that we wouldn't have to serve in the army. So we moved to Manitoba in Canada. We left there in the late 'fifties because the government wanted us to send our children to schools in English. We've been in Belize ever since. While it's not as good for farming as Canada, at least the Government leaves us alone, which is the way we like it."

"What do you believe?"

"We believe in following Christ's example and living a simple, plain life. Following the Anabaptist tradition of our founder Menno Simon, we don't believe in established churches with their ecclesiastical hierarchies and elaborate liturgies. Everyone has a direct personal relationship to God and must choose to join the church. That's why we practice adult baptism. We also believe in non-violence, non-resistance, and community. Put more simply in the Bible's terms, we believe in 'turning the other cheek,' 'loving your enemies,' and 'everybody is their brother's keeper.' For these basic beliefs, we've often been persecuted and forced to flee."

"It's too bad people can't be more tolerant of each other's beliefs," said Bob, exhibiting a newfound philosophical disposition that would have amazed his first two wives and Donna.

Another day Johann took Bob over to see his lumbermill. It was a large barn-like building in a clearing, down the river a few hundred yards from the farm. Inside was a large saw powered by a gasoline engine where two Mennonite men were busy cutting wood into different sized pieces of lumber.

"We are making lumber for houses now. We can also switch over and use our specialty tools such as tumblers, polishers and drills to make components for furniture. There is still some mahogany left in this bush and furniture made from it is very high quality and much in demand in Belize City. We sell it there along Front Street every Friday," said Johann proudly.

"It's all very impressive the technology you've developed here. But I don't understand why you use gas engines in the sawmill, but won't drive cars."

"There's a devil in the motor, which of course we don't like," said Johann, with a twinkle in his eye. "But if it's fastened down like it is in the mill, it can't get out of control and run away on us."

"I see," said Bob, smiling, not sure if Johann was pulling his leg.

A few days later at breakfast, Johann asked Bob if he would like to come along to a barn-raising at a neighbor's farm down the road. The neighbor's name was Mr. Weibe. His family was growing and he needed more room for livestock. Since Bob felt very secure in the tightknit

Mennonite community and wanted to do something to pay them back for their hospitality, he readily agreed. Johann, Bob, and Peter, Johann's oldest son, who was twelve, walked over to join the other men who were already busily at work.

All morning the men labored together putting precut lumber into position to make the four sides of the barn and nailing the pieces together. The main structural beams were also attached using tongue in groove joints. Around noon, the women, in their wide-brimmed straw hats tied on with black scarves and ankle-length print dresses, started to arrive with the children. Some came in buggies and others on foot, but, regardless of how they got there, they all brought dishes of food and laid them out on the long, rough wood tables that had already been put up. When the table was set and covered with a bounty of smoked hams, roast chickens, bean salads, cole slaw, pickled beets, dumplings and an assortment of pies, the men were called to come sit down at the table. Before they started the feast, one of the men, an elder, led them in a traditional Mennonite prayer.

"Grace be with us and peace from Him, Who is, Who was, and Who is to come."

"Amen," responded the assembled group solemnly.

The women served the meal while the hungry men ate and talked and laughed. Once the men were finished, they went back to work. It was then the turn of the women and children to eat their lunch.

In the afternoon, the main task was to attach ropes to the various component sides and raise them, sinking the bases into the foundation holes that had been dug. The sides went up quickly with the men working in unison. Bob tried to be helpful without getting in the way. Then the men climbed all over the structure and nailed on the sideboards and installed the tin roof.

While the men worked, Nick's truck drove by again, but all his men could see were a bunch of Mennonites raising a barn. In these parts, there was nothing unusual about that to arouse their suspicion. When Bob saw the truck, his heart jumped. But when it passed, he knew that he had become indistinguishable from the rest of the community. By dumb luck, he had found the perfect disguise.

At the end of the day, a brand new barn stood where there had been nothing. Bob was exhausted but exhilarated to have participated. As he walked home with Johann and Peter, he said, "I've never seen anything like this. The way your community came together today to help Mr. Weibe. Everyone worked as one. It's like I imagine it used to be in the pioneer days back in Loganville where I come from. It's something that's missing from the modern world where people are selfish and don't have strong ties to each other and the community."

Johann replied, "We help one another. It's just the way we are. It's the way we want to stay."

Later that night, Bob and Johann were sitting in the kitchen drinking coffee while Mia was feeding the baby and the children were getting ready for bed. After they had talked a while about the barn raising, the conversation turned to the Old Colony Mennonite's aversion to technology.

"Why don't you have a TV?" asked Bob.

"Television and radio would have a very destructive effect on our way of life. If we had them, people would stay home and watch TV or listen to the radio rather than visiting their neighbors. It's our constant visiting back and forth that keeps our community close. How can we care for our neighbors if we don't know them and appreciate their problems?" asked Johann.

"You've got a point. People back where I come from have their TVs on all the time. Sometimes when people come over to visit, they just sit there glued to the tube and ignore their company. TV has become a national obsession with people back in the United States. It keeps them at home and socially isolated. But you know, when you come home from a very hard day's work and are all stressed out, it can be very tempting to just sit down in your nice comfortable chair in front of the television and space out. I even do it myself on occasion." Bob was not being wholly truthful here. In fact, it would have been more accurate to say he did it a lot.

Sunday was the high point of the week in the Old Colony Mennonite community. In the morning, everyone gathered for church services. In the afternoon, families visited each other and shared the Sunday meal. Since the Friesens didn't want Bob to feel left out, they invited him to accompany them to church. Out of a combination of politeness and curiosity, he accepted. Johann lent him the appropriate clothing.

After breakfast, Peter and Aron harnessed up the buggy and, all dressed in their Sunday finery, they crowded in for the ride to the church meeting house. It wasn't far. When they got there, the yard outside the white-wood structure was filled with buggies, and families were already entering the church. Johann drove up to the fence next to the other buggies and hitched Gerda to the fencepost. The men, including Bob, were dressed somberly in dark black coats and trousers. The coats with old fashioned cut-away backs were buttoned straight up the front to the neckband and had no collars or lapels. On their heads, they wore broad-brimmed black hats with round crowns. The women had on dark print dresses and black satin bonnets.

Johann took Bob around and introduced him to some of the people he had not met.

"These are my parents, Cornelius and Leah Friesen," said Johann. "My father started the sawmill business, but now he mostly tends his farm."

"Pleased to meet you," said Bob, as they filed into the church.

Inside, the men and women separated and took their places on benches and waited for the service to begin. The church was very simple. At the front was a long, desk-like lectern where five men were seated.

"Those are our preachers," Johann whispered to Bob as they took their seats. "The one in the middle is the Elder. They are all chosen for life by lot. Slips of paper are inserted in the hymnals. Then the books are passed out to all the eligible men. The chosen one is he who gets the book containing the verse which says 'The lot is cast into the lap, but the decision is wholly from the Lord.' It's from Proverbs 16:37."

A chorister came to the front with a copy of the Old Gesangbuch, and led the congregation in singing a hymn in German. In English it went:

> My God! Another day has dawned
> Another night has run its course,
> And all my cares are still around,
> And I no better than at first.
> My sleep is done, I rest no more,
> But I am just where I was before.
> I am still in the Vale of Sorrows,
> Where each day bears its load of pain;
> Where I but heap the eves and morrows
> With sins and misdeed without gain.
> O God! whose food and drink I share!
> Let me be useful and do my share.

The long and slow-paced hymn continued lugubriously for four more verses as the congregation sang in unison. The hymn certainly couldn't compare with the rhythm and vitality of black gospel singing. But the congregation did seem to enjoy singing it just the same.

Toddlers and small children sat with their mothers. Periodically, an embarrassed-looking mother would rush out with a small child that had gotten too unruly. Girls sat together in a row on the women's side, whispering and giggling. Boys sat on the men's side, talking in low voices and occasionally pushing or pulling on each other.

After the hymn, one of the preachers, not the Elder, got up and gave a brief sermon. Afterwards, the congregation turned towards their seats and with their backs to the front of the church knelt together in silent prayer. Once they were done and back in their seats, the Elder got up to give the main sermon. He was a tall, thin man in his sixties with a tanned, weatherbeaten face, which evidenced a life of hard physical work outside in the sun. He did not preach hellfire and damnation like some evangelical ministers back home. Instead, he stressed the virtues of a simple life like the one Christ led. He quoted from St. Paul's epistle to the Romans (12:10) "Mind not high things, but condescend to men of low estate." As he explained, this meant that farming was the best lifestyle for God-fearing people as it represented the lowest estate. He said people may not make much money as farmers, but that wasn't important. Quoting Matthew (16: 26), he asked "What shall it profit a man, if he gains the whole world and forfeits his soul?" Or so went the short English translation that Johann later gave to Bob of what it took the Elder a long time to say in German.

The Elder's sermon was followed by testimonials given by the other preachers. Finally, the Elder concluded the service with a prayer, and the congregation sang another hymn from the hymnal.

Bob looked at his watch as they filed out of the meeting house. The whole service had lasted about two hours. It had been hard for Bob to sit still for that long and watch something he did not fully understand. But he was glad he had come just the same. He had learned something important about people and community. It made the real danger he faced seem distant, giving him a sense, maybe false, of security.

Back at the Friesen's that afternoon, Johann's parents came over as they always did after church. They loved to watch their children and grandchildren grow and in return were the recipients of much love and respect from the younger members of their family. In addition, two other families, the Yoders and the Klassens, who were cousins of some sort, stopped by for a visit. Johann introduced them all to Bob and then took the men around to the barn to show off his new cow and the vegetable garden. The women went into the house with Mia to talk about whatever it was that Mennonite women talk about, while the children played games in the yard. After about an hour, Mia called the men and children to come, and with the help of the women served a sumptuous homestyle dinner of roast chicken, rice and assorted salads and rolls. Following the dinner, the women helped Mia clean up, while they chatted. In the meantime, the men visited some more and the children played. The afternoon passed quickly and everyone was sorry when the time to leave eventually came.

21

The Zion Pentecostal Church was a modest block structure in the south end of town. Only the bottom level of what was to have been a towering spire pointing to heaven had been completed before the money ran out. Donna had passed the church many times driving down Jefferson Street, but this was the first time she had ever been inside. Earl had invited her to come to the regular Sunday morning service he conducted. While she wasn't too keen on churches, she knew that if she was going to get more serious with Earl, she needed to find out who he was and what made him tick. He seemed like a good man, but was he the right man for her?

Donna walked through the door and self-consciously took her place in one of the pews at the back of the church. The choir, which was standing in the front of the church behind a small pulpit, had already started to sing a few hymns, accompanied by an organist. The church was filled and everyone was singing loudly and enthusiastically clapping their hands.

> There are souls in sin that the Lord would win,
> But we only lack desire;
> And the thing we need—sorely need indeed—
> Is the Pentecostal fire.
>
> That's the thing (that's the thing)
> the very thing (the very thing),
> That is what we must acquire;
> Let us pray once more as they prayed of yore
> For the Pentecostal fire.

Occasionally, someone would stand up and raise their hands and voice in praise of the Lord as the hymns rolled fervently on.

Looking very handsome in a light blue suit and red tie, Earl came out from a door to the right of the pulpit. He was carrying a few papers and walked up and put them on the lectern. When he started his sermon, there was a fire in his eyes that Donna had never seen before.

"Welcome, my brothers and sisters in Christ," Earl said. "I can tell by your singing that you're ready to embrace the Lord today. You know that God so loved you that he sent his only begotten son Jesus Christ to die for you and save you from your sins. Do you accept Jesus as your personal savior?"

"Yes, Pastor, yes, we do," came the reply of the congregation.

"Do you unworthy sinners repent your sins?" he said, pointing at a man in the front row.

"Yes, we do," again came the reply growing louder.

"The demon Satan will not leave you alone while you are here on earth," shouted Earl with indignation. "He wants to take you down into the burning pit of Hell where you will be condemned to the eternal fires of damnation. I warn you that the devil will tempt you, but you must resist him. Yet be not proud for salvation is not something you can earn or even deserve. No, it is a gift freely given from God Almighty that only comes to us through the atoning work of Christ and the grace of God."

"Amen," said the congregation. "Praise the Lord!"

"Jesus told us in John 3:5 you must be 'born of the spirit' to enter the Kingdom of God. The full meaning of this is given in Acts 2:1-4, where it is written, 'When the day of Pentecost came, they were all together in one place. Suddenly a sound like the blowing of a violent wind came from heaven and filled the whole house where they were sitting. They saw what seemed to be tongues of fire that separated and came to rest on each of them. All of them were filled with the Holy Spirit and began to speak in other tongues as the Spirit enabled them'."

"You've all been baptized by water and were born again in Christ. But not everyone has been baptized in the Holy Spirit. Do you want this higher form of baptism?" he asked.

"Yes, Pastor," responded a few members of the congregation.

"Do you really want this higher form of baptism? " he shouted.

"Yes, Pastor, yes," yelled back the congregation in unison.

"You see, the evidence of being 'born of the spirit' is speaking in tongues," he preached, adopting a more conversational tone. "This is the gift of tongues. To get it, we have to ask God to grant it to us. Let us all pray together. Repeat after me."

Speaking louder, he began, "Father..., in the name of Jesus..., I ask you now for the Holy Spirit..., fill me with power..., give me what I lack..., and I'll receive the power of the Holy Spirit right now in my life...."

Donna was startled when the man sitting next to her jumped up suddenly and made his way to the front of the church where he stood before the Pastor.

"Praise the Lord, Glory to God!" the congregation shouted in an increasing frenzy.

The Pastor, himself trembling with excitement, laid his hands on the head of one member of the congregation. At the touch, the man keeled over on the floor and started shaking. Next thing he was babbling, while it was impossible for Donna to say exactly what, it sounded to her like, "BANAKU HEHMINKO AI OLAN ZI GETA GONO SIBABELO." The incoherent noises rambled on. Sometimes it sounded like nonsense words. Other times more like the barking or growling of a dog. At first, single file, and then in groups of two or three, members of the congregation marched up for the laying on of hands. Soon more than ten people, men, women and children, were speaking in tongues. Some were on the floor, rolling and tossing. Others were walking around in a daze, ranting unintelligibly. As the number of those speaking in tongues increased, the rest of the congregation got more and more excited and egged them on with shouts of "Praise the Lord" or "Hallelujah" as those possessed of the Holy Ghost flailed their arms about spastically.

Donna, whose only previous exposure to the spirit of religion had been in the staid Presbyterian Church her parents used to drag her to on Sundays as a youth, became increasingly alarmed as the congregation seemed to her to be spinning dangerously out of control. She found the whole over-the-top spectacle to be profoundly disturbing to her sense of decorum. The final straw for her was when Earl himself got up, dripping wet with sweat, and started speaking in tongues from the pulpit. This was more than she could take. She didn't know what she could possibly say to him after such a service which was so unlike anything she had every seen before. A simple, noncommittal "oh, the service was nice" would not suffice. No, she couldn't fake it this time. You either felt the service or you didn't. And she clearly didn't. This made her feel very much the odd person out. Seeing only one way out, she took it. Picking up her purse, she quietly slipped out of church on her tiptoes. Everybody including Earl was so preoccupied with the mayhem that nobody noticed her departure.

The Golden Arches were beckoning and it wasn't the Gates to Heaven. It was a couple of days later and Donna and Connie were sitting at a table by the window having a quick lunch together at the McDonald's on the northern strip as they often did. It was conveniently close both to Donna's house and to the real estate office where Connie worked as a secretary. And though both of them were too ashamed to admit it, they loved to indulge themselves with tasty high-fat, high-cholesterol food. This was a habit they developed when their children were younger and in the thrall of McDonald's heavy duty, kid-oriented marketing program. Sarah and Jessica would gobble down their Happy Meals with relish and rush off to cavort in Playland, while their mothers leisurely dined and sipped coffee in fine McDonald's style, much relieved to be, if only temporarily, liberated from their demanding toddlers.

"One of these days, we should try one of their salads," said Connie guiltily as she opened up the red paper box containing a Big Mac.

"I don't see on the sign where it says a zillion salads sold," wisecracked Donna, opening her own Big Mac.

After glancing at a pamphlet on dietary information she had obtained from one of the earnest young kids working behind the counter of the world's largest fast-food empire, Connie asked, "Did you know that a Big Mac contains 590 calories and a large French fries 540 calories?"

"Ple...ease," said Donna, "Don't spoil my lunch. We can take in an extra aerobics class this week to work it off and keep our girlish figures."

"You're gonna need yours if you're going to catch Earl," joked Connie, taking a big bite out of her hamburger.

"Uh-uh, ...I'm afraid that's not gonna work out. I'm sorry to disappoint you but...I won't be trying to catch Earl anymore...if I ever was."

"What's the matter?" asked Connie. "He's a good man. Isn't he?"

"Yes, he certainly is. In some respects, better than any I've ever known. But he's definitely not the man for me. We're too different, Earl and I. He's...er...too religious."

"Too religious, what are you talking about? He's a minister. He's supposed to be religious. There's nothing wrong with that. They get paid like everyone else. And a little church never hurt anyone. In fact it would probably do you some good."

"That's fine for you to say, but what do you know about his church?" shot back Donna vehemently. "They're fundamentalists, Bible thumpers, Jesus freaks. Call them what you want. They're zealots. They rant and rave and speak in tongues."

"I don't know what you're so upset about. At least they don't handle snakes," laughed Connie.

"Don't joke, Connie. I'm serious. Their church services are way too much for me, especially since I'm not even sure what I believe. I prefer my religion in a much more sedate and liberal package, just like you like hotdogs better than tamales when you go to the A&W."

"You told Earl how you feel?" asked Connie.

"Not exactly in those terms. I tried to let him down gently."

"What are you gonna do now? Mope around and hope Bob comes back?"

"No, I'm gonna go down to Belize and get him and bring him back one way or the other. I've already bought the ticket and I'm leaving first thing tomorrow morning."

"Boy, you have really flipped out. I don't know if Bob's worth all the trouble and expense, assuming of course you can get him to come back if you do happen to find him."

"Well, if I can't sweet talk him back, I can always drag him by the ear. Bob may not be as nice as Earl, but I know he accepts me as I am and he's not gonna try to change me. We've been together a long time and we're comfortable together. I'm sure we can work things out. Who knows? Maybe that's what love really is.

"Well, so much for the Harlequin Romance view of the world we used to have back in high school," mused Connie philosophically.

"Will you check in on Sarah while I'm gone?" asked Donna.

"Of course," said Connie. "You know you can always count on me. That's what friends are for."

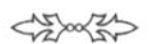

The next morning at 7 o'clock Donna was rushing to the airport in her little Honda Civic. The plane left in a half hour and she was running late. There had been a few last-minute instructions she had had to write down for Sarah. It was a big step for her to leave Sarah by herself. But Donna consoled herself that Sarah was getting pretty old and Connie would keep an eye on her and try to keep her out of trouble. She was determined to find Bob. Maybe, she thought, they would even be able to have a romantic little vacation together on that island down there Bob talked about. What was the name of it? Greasy Key or something like that? She had brought along a couple of bikinis and some beach towels for lying on the beach. It was going to be fun, she hoped.

Donna turned right onto the Airport Road. The engine in her car started to sputter. She pushed on the accelerator and the car jerked ahead spasmodically and then slowed. She pushed again—same troublesome response.Damn, she thought as the car coasted off to the side of the road. Why does this car always break down just when I need it most? What am I going to do now? It's already a quarter after eight. And here I am stuck by the side of the road with one of those cheap nonrefundable airline tickets. Better call Connie on the cell phone. She dialed the familiar number.

"Hi, Connie," Donna said.

"Where are you? I thought you were supposed to be on the plane to Belize."

"Yeah, well, the car finally self-destructed and left me stranded out on Airport Road."

"What do you want me to do?" Connie asked.

"Could you come and take me to the airport? I've still got fifteen minutes."

"Who do you think I am, Dale Earnhardt? There's no way I can get there that fast."

"Well, then, maybe you could just come and pick me up and take me home," Donna said, starting to cry.

"Oh, honey, I'm sorry. What are you gonna do now?"

"I guess now that I've blown all my money on a nonrefundable ticket, there's nothing left for me to do except sit around and wait for him to come back."

"I'll keep you company."

"Thanks, you're a real true friend."

22

The next morning when he woke up, Bob lay in bed thinking and taking stock. He felt healthy again and longed to go home. Sure, it was nice to stay with the Friesens. Their close-knit family and community and the love they shared revitalized him. But as long as he was in Belize and so close to Nick's plantation, his life was definitely in danger. If Nick's men, who had already driven by two times in their truck, were to get their hands on him, he shuddered at the thought of what they might do to him for taking the jade head, not to speak of what he knew of Nick's business affairs. In addition, the time had come to get on with his own life. He couldn't hide out forever in Belize. He still had Donna and his kids back home, and, of course, the jade head. His first problem though was getting out of Belize. Nick would still be looking for him. The airport would be the obvious place for him to go. Nick must have it staked out by some of his men.

At the usual hearty breakfast at the Friesen's with all the children seated around the table while Mia served the food, Bob told Johann how he felt.

"I'm better now and should be going. I don't want to impose on your hospitality too long."

"You're welcome to stay as long as you want," said Johann sincerely.

"I know," said Bob. "And don't think I don't appreciate all you and Mia have done for me. But I have to go home. I've been away from home far too long."

"I understand," said Johann, nodding.

"But I'm afraid I'm still gonna need some more of your help. How can I get to the airport?"

"I can take you out to the Northern Highway in the buggy. There's a bus stop nearby. You can catch a Batty Bus to take you into Ladyville near the airport. They run every half hour or so in the morning."

"I have an open return ticket home although the ink on it is smeared a bit from a little swim I took in the river. Can I get to the airport in time to catch a one o'clock plane?"

"I can take you out as soon as we finish eating. It will only take a couple of hours to get there. You can be there in plenty of time."

After Bob said good-bye to Mia and the family, he and Johann got in the black buggy and headed for the highway. All his things were in a bulging plastic shopping bag on the seat next to him. When they got to the bus stop, Bob shook Johann's hand and thanked him profusely for everything he had done. Of all the people he had met in his life, Johann was the closest to a saint, perhaps an anachronism in the modern secular world, but no less authentic. Bob's eyes were misty as he climbed down for he knew he probably would never see Johann again.

As he turned the buggy around, Johann said, "May God be with you."

"And you, too," said Bob, the solemnity of the occasion making him act and feel more religious than he actually was. Better be careful, Bob thought, as he watched the buggy recede down the road, or the next thing I'll be getting Jesus.

Bob didn't have to wait long before a Batty Bus pulled up and stopped. The appearance of this dilapidated piece of late twentieth century automotive engineering heralded his return to the modern world, or at least a step closer to the industrial society.

"You goin' to Belize, maan?" the gap-toothed Creole driver asked.

"No, the airport," replied Bob.

"All de same. Clim' in, maan," the driver said.

As soon as Bob got in the bus, he was overcome by loud cacophonous music. Sitting down in an empty seat in the middle, he could hear two men arguing in the back of the bus. A big Creole man was shouting at a little Mestizo playing Spanish music "Shot op de cassette. Put down de fockin' Spanish cassette. Den we can hear de wireless." His ferocity must have been very intimidating because the mariachi music on the cassette player immediately stopped, and the voice of Shaba Ranks singing "Ting-A-Ling" came through loud and clear on the radio.

The bus was filled with a mixed crowd of Mestizos and Creoles going to Belize City for the weekend. Some were sugar cane workers, others farmers, or workers with their families. There were many children on the bus and even a few chickens on their way to the Belize market. Bob was the only one that looked like a Mennonite and, needless to say, there were no American tourists riding in the crowded, un-air-conditioned bus.

The bus left Bob at the entrance to the airport. Holding his heavy plastic bag in his hand, he walked in, following the dirt path next to the road. When he got to the front of the terminal, he could see a suspicious-looking man wearing sunglasses, tan slacks and a burgundy guayabera, leaning on the wall next to the door. The gold chain around his neck was of the type favored by the fashionable young toughs that Nick surrounded himself with. Uh-oh, thought Bob, trouble.

Steeling himself, Bob pulled his straw hat down and walked by, trying not to look the man in the face. To his great relief, the strategy worked swimmingly. The man paid absolutely no attention to him whatsoever. I must really look like a Mennonite, he thought. It's incredible. People don't pay any attention to them at all. It's like they're not even there. It's like being an invisible man.

Inside the terminal, Bob went over to the American Airline ticket counter and presented his weather-beaten ticket. He was in luck. The young uniformed Belizean women working behind the counter accepted it without making much of a fuss since it was recorded on the airline's computerized reservation system. Fortunately for Bob, Flight 2104 to Miami was not fully booked that day. The woman didn't even seem to be put off by the fact that all his belongings were in a carry-on plastic bag. Bob showed her his passport. It looked pretty good. There was little water damage. The picture was another story. It showed Bob wearing a coat and tie. But the ticket clerk didn't seem to be troubled by the fact that he was now dressed like a Mennonite in an old baggy black suit. Apparently Belizeans were used to eccentric tourists dressing in all sorts of strange ways and take little note one way or the other. She just told him the flight would be boarding in forty-five minutes and he could proceed through security whenever he liked. She wished him a pleasant flight.

Bob went over immediately to security as he was anxious to put the security gate between himself and the man he thought worked for Nick. He showed the security guard his ticket and put his heavy plastic bag on the conveyor belt. As there was no metal in it, it set off no alarms. Passing through the metal detector, he picked up his package and went over to sit down. A *Miami Herald* was laying on the table next to him. Almost automatically, he picked it up and began thumbing through it. It had been weeks since he had heard any news of the outside world, which to him, of course, meant the good old US of A. His mind started to wander in anticipation. It would be good to get home again. He hoped Donna would be real happy to see him. He realized that he hadn't kept in touch like he should have, but he would try to make it up to her now that he had something more to give.

Two uniformed Belizean policemen came into the waiting room. They had a German shepherd dog with them. The dog was coming directly over to him. Bob's heart started beating fast. What was the dog looking for? Drugs. He didn't have any. The dog came right up to him with its tongue hanging out and put its head in his crotch and took a big sniff. Then it moved on to the next person and repeated the procedure. What is it with that dog? thought Bob. It's not going to find any drugs doing that.

American Airlines Flight 2104 was called over the public address system. Bob lined up at the gate with his plastic shopping bag in hand and newspaper under his arm and presented his ticket. Then he walked out the door onto the tarmac. The sun beat down and the ripe, almost rotten, smell of tropical vegetation again filled his nostrils with every breath. But he didn't even notice. He had become accustomed to the heat and smell of Belize.

Inside the plane, Bob took his assigned seat 18A near the window and carefully put his plastic bag under the seat in front of him. A middle-aged man in a tropical suit sporting a goatee sat down next to him. Bob fastened his seat belt and waited for the plane to taxi out on the runway and take off. It didn't take long. Not like O'Hare, where the planes are lined up for miles, occasioning long waits.

The plane roared down the runway and soon was airborne. As it circled and gained altitude, Bob could see Belize City receding below in the distance. In a few more minutes, they passed over Ambergrise Caye. Bob wished he could have said good-bye to some of the wonderful people he had met: Wally, Gideon, Dr. Butterfield, Neville Jones, and Pedro Uck. But the circumstances of his departure didn't allow it. And sadly would also prevent him from ever returning to this marvelous and varied country. But most of all, he would grieve Luna. He blamed himself a lot for what had happened to her. He should have heeded the warnings and listened to the voice of caution within himself. Then he could have prevented her death. But he knew that, wherever she may be now, she would be happy that at least they had managed to get the jade head away from that no-good bastard Nick.

The voice of the goateed man sitting next to Bob interrupted the free flow of his thoughts. "Since we're going to be sitting together, I should introduce myself," he said. "My name is Dr. Edward Pemberton. I'm an archeologist from Trent University in Canada."

"My name is Bob Wayne. I'm a tourist from Illinois. Strange, I keep running into Canadian archeologists down here. Aren't there any archeological sites in Canada you can excavate? Or are they all frozen?"

"No, only half the year, but, even when they're not frozen, they're nothing like the Mayan sites," Dr. Pemberton said, his face lighting up at the opportunity to talk about his favorite subject. "What about you, are you interested in Mayans?"

"Er...I guess...maybe a little."

"Well, then, perhaps when you get back to Illinois, you might want to go see the exhibit of Mayan artifacts at the Art Institute of Chicago. They are going to have the famous jade statue of the Sun God, Kinich Ahau, on loan from the Department of Archeology in Belmopan. I hear it's spectacular. You can read all about it in that *Miami Herald* you have in your lap."

"No, I think I'll take a pass on that. I've had enough of jade heads," said Bob cryptically, opening up his paper. "Now if you'll excuse me, I'd like to catch up on the news."

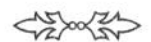

A horse-drawn buggy pulled up to the Post Office on Main Street in Orange Walk; a Mennonite man walked in carrying a heavy square box about seven inches in all dimensions wrapped in paper and tied with a string. He paid the postal clerk for the required postage and then went back to his buggy and rode off. The package was addressed to the Department of Archeology, Belmopan, Belize. Inside was the jade head of Ixchel, the moon goddess, which, as a national treasure, was being returned to its rightful owners, the people of Belize. Also enclosed was a letter to be forwarded to the Chief of the National Police Force, detailing all that Bob could remember about Nick's criminal activities, including his illegal forays into archeology. Hopefully, Nick would get what was coming to him. But if not, at least he no longer had the jade head in his foul clutches.

Sitting in the plane, staring blankly at the newspaper, Bob thought about where his life was headed. While he had only been in Belize a few months, and he wouldn't have put it this way, he had been born again, not exactly as a Christian, but as a human being who cared for others and was beginning to feel at peace with himself and his own lot in life.

I'm going to try to take life one day at a time and only worry about what really matters, he thought. This means taking more joy from simple things and not expecting so much. I sure hope Donna will still be there waiting. I know that may be too much to expect. I couldn't blame her if she wasn't, though. God, I acted like a macho fool. Fuck all that Ernest Hemingway stuff! I pray it's not too late.

At midnight, the newly redeemed Bob was standing outside Donna's bungalow, trying to get up his nerve to knock on the door. He was shivering in the late fall cold. Or was it in anticipation? Will she be glad to see me? he asked himself. Or have I once again blown it through my own stupidity? He knocked on the door softly at first, but got no response. He tried a little harder and a dog started barking.

"Jesus Christ," he said. "I forgot all about Toto."

The light went on in the back of the house. Bob could hear Donna's voice.

"Down, Toto, down," she said, as the dog jumped on her excitedly barking.

In what took only a few seconds, but seemed like an hour to Bob, the door opened a crack with the chain still on.

"Yes," she said in a sleepy voice.

"It's me, Donna. I've come home."

"Oh! Bob, I was worried you were gone for good," she said, opening the door.

She pulled him into the hallway shutting the door on the night's cold and turning on the light.After a passionate embrace, they stepped back awkwardly to look at each other. She was standing there in her old flannel nightgown with little yellow flowers. He was still wearing the floppy straw hat and baggy black suit Johann had given him.

"What in the world?" she said, taking a closer look. "What are you supposed to be?"

"I'll tell you all about it later, everything, and you can tell me what's happened to you. But first I have something important to say."

"Bob, you look so much thinner and tanned. What have you been doing?"

"I've got to tell you something first."

"What?"

"Donna, I don't know how to say this, but I've realized you were the best thing in my life. I've treated you unfairly and I want to make it up to you."

"What are you saying, Bob?"

"I'm saying it wasn't fair the way I ran away from everything and just walked out on you. You deserve much better than that. I'm really sorry. I'll try to make it up to you, I promise. We can still have many years together.

"What do you mean?"

"I've realized that Loganville is my home and that's where I want to live and leave my mark. I'll put out my shingle as an accountant. Why not? People know me in the town. Hell, some people like Carl, Jim and Sam even like me. I'm not such a bad guy. I'm sure there will be enough work. I won't get rich, but I can at least make an honest living for us to get by and keep our creditors at bay. I won't need flashy luxuries like that damn Mustang anymore."

At the mention of the Mustang, she said, "I have something to tell you, too, but it can wait until later."

"You smashed it. Didn't you?" he asked.

"Yes," she said, looking down.

"Don't worry, honey. It doesn't matter to me anymore. What's important is being able to share my life with you and our family. I want to help you with Sarah. And I need to get closer to my kids while I still can. If I can't love my own kids, who can I love? Maybe you can help me to get back in their lives."

"You sound different to me. Are you sure you're all right?"

Throughout this long true confession, Toto had stood by uncharacteristically silent, perhaps bewildered by Bob's strange costume and weird behavior.

"And one final thing."

"What?"

"Will you marry me?"

Sarah's voice came from the other room. "Who's that, Mom?"

"It's Bob. He's back and asked me to marry him."

"Well, tell him yes," Sarah said, running over to give Bob a big hug and causing Toto to start barking again.

"Don't worry. I will," said Donna, putting her arm around both Sarah and Bob. "But first I want to give him a few days to make sure he hasn't gone loco."

That sounded as good as a "yes" to Bob's waiting ears. It was sure great to be home again where he belonged. He had learned that life is not like golf—you only have one shot and you've got to make the best of it. And he was making the best of his, even if his ball never seemed to go straight.

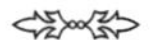